PIRATE SHIRT DOT COM

Shannon M. Risk

Best Wishes!
Shannon Risk

PublishAmerica
Baltimore

First printing

At the specific preference of the author, PublishAmerica allowed this work to remain exactly as the author intended, verbatim, without editorial input.

ISBN: 1-4241-5399-9
PUBLISHED BY PUBLISHAMERICA, LLLP
www.publishamerica.com
Baltimore

Printed in the United States of America

For my parents, Ella and Malcolm Risk.

I

"Good morning. Pirate Shirt Dot Com." Susana Hammond, in mid-swing, caught her shoe on the miniature wastebasket by her desk, dumping out a million little paper-hole punch holes onto the crème Berber carpet. She stuck out her other foot, attempting to move paper holes across the carpet and back to the base of the wastebasket. She succeeded only in grinding some of the paper holes into the carpet, while others caught wind and drifted further away. Some of the paper holes had the audacity to actually dig into the grooves on the soles of her shoes. She threw her left hand up in the air, vowing to get out the vacuum once this phone call was handled.

"Yes, you have the right place. We arrange for our clients to have romantic outings, whether it is an adventure on the high seas, as our company name suggests, or something perhaps a bit more subtle." Susana twirled her red hair, nodding into the phone.

"Yep, yep, we do that…yes, that too…no, I wouldn't call us a travel agency exactly," Susana said and resumed turning her office chair around in circles. "Well, we are really in the *romantic adventure* business. We get a lot of calls from clients, who want to put together an anniversary dinner for their spouse, and after that, they are so pleased; they continue to engage us for special dates.

Others use our services to propose to their fiancés." Susana stopped twirling in her chair and switched her attention to balancing her pen on the back of her phone-free hand.

The front door swung open and a good-looking young man with a tool belt walked in. Susana sized him up immediately and decided he was "yummy." He was, in fact, so "yummy" that she could no longer balance her pen on the back of her hand and carry on a phone conversation. Her hand spasmed and the pen flew across the room, miraculously marking a line of ink across the forehead of yummy tool belt guy. Meanwhile, the paper holes scattered even further as a cool late May breeze floated in. Yummy tool belt guy, still stunned from being branded by Susana's pen, shut the door in haste, shaking the hinges.

Susana, now a nice shade of pink to compliment her copper-fire locks, put up a shaky finger to indicate that the man should wait for a moment while she wrapped up the call.

"Yes, well I can send you our press kit to see what we have to offer. We do have romantic packages but we can also assemble an event for you a la carte. Great! Let me get your address." Susana fumbled around for a pen and then remembered; it was somewhere across the room, probably lodged in her older sister, Sophie's bouquet of her favorite flowers, bird of paradise. Yummy tool belt guy smiled broadly and pulled a pen out of his front pocket— not his tool belt—and held it out to Susana, who attempted a grateful, yet still humiliated smile.

"Terrific. I'll send this press packet out to you right away. I think you'll be impressed by what we have to offer. Goodbye." Susana scribbled down the rest of the caller's information and hung up the phone.

"Hello!" She said much too brightly. "Can I help you?" Her "inner dialogue" as she and Sophie called it, said, *Can I help you...yummy tool belt guy?* Thank goodness her inner dialogue did not completely run her life—at least not yet.

"Yes, hi, the name is Nathan Lake—um, I mean, Nate—and I'm working on that house down at the end of the street." He motioned arbitrarily out beyond the front door. Now he was embarrassed.

"Oh, right, that beautiful Victorian that is getting re-worked?" Susana cooed, trying very hard not to sound like she was making an effort.

"Uh, yes, the word we use is 'refurbished'." He put his hands at his tool belt, unsure what to do or say next.

Fortunately, Susana was the queen of small talk. Despite her talents, however, the pink was creeping further still up her face. "Please," she waved her hand over to the chairs (because Mother always said pointing was rude), "take a seat and make yourself comfortable. Can I get you a coffee or water?" He shook his head no, moving stiffly over to the lounge beyond Susana's desk.

"That house is just gorgeous. What exactly are you working on there?" She leaned forward at her desk, praying that he wouldn't see the ink stain, the mustard stain, and the tear in her white blouse. She'd obviously forgotten to pay the gravity bill this month, as everything today seemed attracted to her shirt, including the doorknob, which earlier that morning, caught and ripped her blouse right at the buttons at her bosom. *Classy*, her inner dialogue sarcastically said.

Nate grinned, happy to have something to say. Susana noticed his eyes crinkled at the corners and his eyebrows went up, as did his ruddy cheekbones. His blond hair was sun-tinged but he wasn't completely tan, which told her he worked mostly indoors. She saw him cup his hands at his knees, attempting gentility as he spoke. Nice, strong hands leading to well-muscled forearms. *Oh boy.*

"I'm working on all parts of the house. I'm currently installing the plumbing, but I'm building new cabinets for the kitchen at my home workshop too. When I first looked at the plumbing, it was a mess. It looked like it hadn't been updated since the 1800s or something." His voice trailed off as if he realized he was going on too long.

"But anyway, I usually drive by this house and it seems to be from the same era as the one I'm working on at the end of the street. And I..." he paused, not quite sure how to continue, "...I wondered if it might be okay if I looked around in here to see how the plumbing system is set up?"

"Oh, sure! No problem!" Susana said, cringing at the sound of her own chirping voice.

"I'm Susana, by the way. I'm the administrative assistant here." She rose with her arms folded in front of her shirt, looking rather awkward, but trying to be graceful.

"Oh, yes, I've seen you out on the front porch reading," Nate said, following behind her as she led him into the kitchen at the back of the house.

"Are there others who live here too? I think I saw a tall woman mowing the lawn one day. And there was a small, dark-haired woman, very professional looking, getting into a car this morning..." He realized he must sound like a stalker.

"Not that I'm a stalker," he said quickly, flashing a smile.

Susana inwardly swooned. "Oh no, of course not!"

She led him into the kitchen and flicked on the light. "I thought we could start here and then I can show you the bathroom and the pipes down in the basement if you'd like." He knelt down and opened the cabinet under the sink.

Getting back to his question, Susana rocked on her *rather stylish* summer strappy sandals, licking her lips. "That tall woman you saw, was my older sister Sophie. You might have also noticed her jogging through the neighborhood. She likes to exercise all the time. And she's working on her PhD in history at the university. She spends a lot of her time reading very obscure books. Some of it's interesting, but some of it looks like torture. I don't know how she does it, but then, she really wants to be a university professor." She grimaced, realizing that she must be babbling.

"And the other woman?" Nate asked, crawling further under the sink with his flashlight.

"Yes, that's Gabby. She's my sister's best friend. They met back in their master's degree programs. Gabby is our business brain. She runs our website and the accounting books. We would have full meltdown without her around!" Susana walked over and stood a bit closer to Nate to see what he was looking at.

"You also have some old pipes back here. In fact, one is pretty badly corroded. You might want to get that fixed."

"Oh, sure, I'll let my sister know." Susana said, thinking she'd never herself crawl under a sink to fix something.

"I'm sorry! How rude of me to just show up and start telling you that your plumbing needs work! I'm sure these pipes will last a while longer," Nate said, inching back out from under the sink.

"Oh, not to worry. Sophie is on top of everything. She'll appreciate hearing about it."

Nate looked around the kitchen, gazing at the movie posters and the brightly colored mugs and plates on the shelves.

"This," Susana whirled around, temporarily forgetting about the tear in the front of her blouse, "Is my design. I mean, I just got my bachelor's degree in fashion merchandising, but I do have a knack for colors—I mean, things other than clothing." She licked her lips, realizing too late that she was eyeing yummy...oops, "Nate."

"Well, you do have a knack for it!" Nate said enthusiastically. "I like the movie posters; they all show the old classic movies where the hero and heroine embrace. And look at their fancy costumes."

"Yeah, I chose those images because of the business we're in here. I figured it would be inspiring to anyone who entered our kitchen!"

"So, do you really run a dating agency? Do you get a lot of customers?" Nate said, leaning against the counter, fascinated at this enterprising house of women.

"Yeah, we do, as far away as Boston. And we had a German tourist last year that had us set up a whole week of romantic activities in the area for her and her husband. Our website really pays off. Plus, Sophie is gone almost every weekend during the winter and spring at college fairs and business expos around New England advertising Pirate Shirt Dot Com." Susana suddenly remembered the tear in her blouse and her hand shot up to cover it, much too quickly.

"And who thought of the title for your company?" Nate asked, now relaxed and taking in this whimsical woman.

"Well, it's hard to get the exact story out of Gabby and Sophie. They tell me different things and then wink at each other. It's annoying!" she said laughing, "but from what I can tell, they got a bit too far into a bottle of Cabernet Sauvignon one night. It was sometime near graduation when they were pondering their futures. They began to joke about pitiful dates they'd been on in the past and somehow, out of the ashes of their drunken conversation, Pirate Shirt Dot Com was born. I've only been working here a few weeks, but the business has been around for a year now."

Susana balanced again on the backs of her *fabulous* summer strappy sandals while yummy admired the movie posters. Just then, the phone rang and she was reminded that she was still on the clock.

"Oh, I'll let that go to the answering machine, but here, let's go see the hall bathroom and the basement. I apologize for the rush," she said, directing him down the hall, wondering if her skirt flattered her back end at all. Probably there was a tuft of cat hair from one of their two cats, Bobo and Mitzi, sticking to her bottom like a rabbit tail. Stranger things had already happened to her that morning, after all.

"I see that you're busy. I'm sorry to have taken up so much time. I could come back closer to quitting time, if that would be better?" Nate said, straightening his tool belt, looking into Susana's blue eyes. She melted.

"Yes…um, yes, terrific. Why don't you do that? It was a pleasure to meet you. And, hey, we're hosting a lawn party in a few weeks." Susana grabbed a postcard for the event from her desk and thrust it out in front of him. "You are more than welcome to stop by. And bring some of your friends! We have many single female clients that will be in attendance. Country club casual dress is preferred," Susana lowered her head, "according to the dictates of my sister." That pesky inner dialogue resurfaced. *But you, yummy tool belt guy, can wear whatever you want!*

"Thanks," Nate said nodding, "I will try to make it." He headed towards the door, but paused and took a look back at Susana. He waved hurriedly and walked out, the door slamming behind him in the wind. The paper holes flew out into the main hallway. The pen lay in its own pool of ink near the front door. But Susana did not notice. She simply stared at the closed door; her heart pounding two hundred beats a minute.

II
_____

"Hi, I'm Sophie Hammond from Pirate Shirt Dot Com." Sophie leaned in closer to the woman seated at the registration table. A banner behind the woman read: *Welcome! Bienvenue! Nashua, New Hampshire Business Expo.* The woman located Sophie's nametag and pulled out a pile of multi-colored forms.

"Here is your registration packet. And," the woman pulled out a floor map of the convention center, "here is where your table is stationed, table 5-A, next to the hotdog stand."

Sophie smiled diplomatically. *How appropriate,* her inner dialogue grumbled, *for a romantic adventure company to be placed right next to a stand selling "wieners." Goody!*

"That sounds fine." Sophie gathered up the various forms and set out to find her table. She sniffed the air, expecting the smell of hot dogs to lure her to table 5-A. She needn't have bothered. About fifty yards ahead was a fifteen-foot plastic inflated hotdog, not completely fastened down, and hovering dangerously over another booth with an exposed barbequing grille. Sophie quietly chuckled. Every weekend was the same thing. Enterprising people in twenty-year-old leisure suits draping their booths with plastic tablecloths and balloons, their business signs either hand-made or put on a cheap banner and duct-taped to the front of their table. Thank goodness this was the last convention of the season.

Gingerly towing a dolly cart loaded with her booth accessories, Sophie came to a halt in front of a dilapidated table with a piece of large masking tape stuck to it that read, Table 5-A. She began to unpack the various items, unfolding a screen that cradled the back of the table. On the screen she had placed hooks, which she used to fasten prints of happy couples on romantic adventures in boats, in the forest, at a restaurant, in a small airplane over Acadia National Park, or viewing an old monastery. Her wooden sign was placed at the center of the screen and read: *Pirate Shirt Dot Com: Where Romantic Adventure Begins!* She then pulled out a pirate shirt that resembled the one comedian Jerry Seinfeld had reluctantly worn on the advice of his friend, Cosmo Kramer, in order to "get women." It was, like the title of her business, a big joke, meant to inspire a humorous double take by the average passerby. Thanks to the talents of her sister, Susana, Sophie was armed today with colorful drapes that she placed over the back of the screen. On the table in front, she spread out another drape her sister had made, with fitted corners and golden tassels. On the table, she put smaller prints of couples in castles, on motorcycles, or chastely positioned in bathtubs. Sophie also put out an easel that held a menu card showing some of their most popular romantic packages and she arranged smaller take-away menus at the sides and middle of the table. *There. Just tacky enough to work!*

With the construction of her booth completed, Sophie allowed herself to survey the convention hall. The floating hotdog had been corralled over the hotdog stand and the aproned purveyor was quickly whipping up fresh hotdogs for convention attendees who were now spilling in. Sophie, wearing a custom-made suit, in a shade of lavender that complimented her dark brown hair and brown yes, not to mention her curvy figure, prepared herself for the litany of public reaction to her business.

For example:

> Question: "So, can you send a couple of girls up to
> my hotel room later?"
> Answer: "No, we are a romantic adventure
> company."

Or worse still –

> Question: "Hey Miss Tall Drink of Water
> (pronounced "Watuh" in typical New England
> fashion)—let's grab a drink and then maybe a little,
> you know?" (Sophie always pictured the Monty
> Python comedy sketch where one man is trying to
> solicit another man's wife by using conversational
> code: Know what I mean? Know what I mean? Say
> no more. Say no more. Wink, wink. Nudge, nudge).
> Answer: Silence and eyes narrowed.

Perhaps it would be different this time. Maybe men would
behave themselves. Perhaps elderly females, who passed by,
wouldn't treat her like the Anti-Christ. Just possibly convention
attendees would understand immediately what her business was
all about. Just for once, parents might not drag their children away
from her booth, while pulling out garlic necklaces and putting
their index fingers together in the form of the Cross. But her inner
dialogue schooled her: *That would be too easy.*

Sophie was jaded. She had been attending conventions and
school expos now for a year. When she and her best friend,
Gabby, dreamed up this scheme, this was one of her brilliant ideas
to get the word out. At that time, she and Gabby agreed that
Sophie would do the face-to-face, meet-and-greet events and

Gabby would handle all Internet applications and accounting. That meant that Gabby never had to fend off the middle-aged man in the afore-mentioned leisure suit, his hair slicked back with foul-smelling Grecian formula, his breath reeking of some kind of whiskey. Sophie had had her "personal" space invaded many times by such a creature.

But wait, who was that over there? Certainly not a slithering polyester gorilla! He was still setting up his booth, which allowed Sophie to spy on him undetected, except, of course, by the hotdog vendor who was pointing at the inflated hotdog, then pointing to her, and then raising his eyebrows. *Know what I mean? Say no more!* Sophie wrinkled her brow and tried her best to ignore the lewd gestures of the hotdog man. She retreated behind her booth table and pretended to arrange the company literature, stealing glances over to the perfectly-normal-what-the-heck-is-he-doing-here-man's booth. He brought out his sign and unfolded it. A sandwich sign. Sophie wondered if she could slam hotdog man in the sandwich sign? Perhaps not.

The sign read: Wild Ride Flying Lessons.

Sophie did a double take. *Wild Ride Flying Lessons!* Ugh, she thought, what a dirty mind she had. (She couldn't, however, admit Pirate Shirt Dot Com was a literary masterpiece—more a drunken farce). The man proceeded to unpack a costume, including a leather bomber jacket, a white aviation scarf, pilot goggles, tan pants, and high boots. Sophie's heart sank into her stomach. *Oh no. Still a pervert, just in a more convincing package.* She turned her gaze away from the handsome man who was now attaching his tan britches over his blue jeans by snap buttons. She began inwardly berating herself for ever launching her Internet business. Really, her job destination would be college professor. Not convention center vamp!

17

The day wore on, Sophie honing her diplomacy skills, handing out quite a lot of brochures to kindly elderly ladies, not one of them yelling: "Witch! Burn her!" *Thank heavens.* She knew it was mostly a waste of materials, but she wanted it to seem that her booth was interesting. And some of these older women actually called the office to follow up. Meanwhile, hotdog guy was mostly too busy to make perverted hand signs and Mr. Wild Ride was demonstrating lift, drag, and pull, with a plastic bi-plane to a family with two boys. In his aviator get-up, he really did look like he could be the Red Baron or something. And he really did move with a certain kind of grace. *Well,* she thought, *the kind of grace that requires tan pants that snap on.*

The convention came to a close and Sophie gladly took a seat. She had stood on her feet all day and her energy was waning. She checked her purse to make sure her pills were still there. She would quickly disassemble her booth and then head back to the hotel restaurant where she could swallow her pain pills with a glass of water. Her feet were aching now, pain impulses bouncing off her big toe knuckles. For a brief moment, she felt dejected, reminded that she was not really the healthy and youthful woman that people saw. But the moment passed quickly because Sophie willed it so. She would not give over one more minute of her life to being distressed because of this illness. She fixed a smile on her face and began taking down her sign and graphics.

Back at the hotel, Sophie changed out of her business suit and into a swimsuit. Her energy was almost gone, but she vowed to swim a few laps. On her way down the stairs, she heard music and voices coming from the hotel bar and she glanced inside as she breezed by. Perhaps she would grab a drink there later.

The swimming pool was small but empty. Sophie tried not to think about the many different strains of urine that the chlorine had to battle every day. She eased into the water, slowly soaking her hair. And then she began swimming. The first laps were always a little tender on her aching joints, but when she was "warmed up," she was more enthusiastic about the venture. Before she knew it, she had swum back and forth fifty times. She coasted to the side of the pool and relaxed, letting her pulse even out. Feeling much better, she rose from the pool and grabbed her towel. It was then that she realized she had forgotten her special swimming towel—the one made for Amazons that she often brought along with her on these business trips. Instead, Sophie had the small hotel-issued towel made for the tiniest of infant babies. In fact, it seemed more like a handkerchief. She dabbed at her hair with the towel and then attempted to wrap it around her body. She could barely pull the sides together at her chest. Grumbling, she threw on her dry clothes, aware that a big wet spot was seeping into the bottom and crotch of her sweatpants.

Sophie headed for the hallway that led to her room—but not soon enough. With impeccable timing, Mr. Wild Ride, the aviator extraordinaire, stepped in front of her on his way to the bar. He stopped suddenly, his eyes riveted to her wet midsection. Sophie picked up the bandage the hotel called a "towel" and held it over her crotch region.

"Uh, hello," she said, trying to sound adult and professional.

"Hi." Mr. Wild Ride was grasping for words, for language that could sanitize the scene before him. "Did you have a nice swim?"

"Did she!" Suddenly, hot dog vendor man appeared out of nowhere, the stench of booze filling the air. "Back and forth, back and forth. She's quite an energetic girly, aren't ya?" Hot dog vendor guy slinked in closer to Sophie. She inched closer to the wall.

"Well, I'm glad I caught you. Remember, you promised me you'd have a drink with me tonight?" Mr. Wild Ride could have been wearing a knight's armor at that precise moment.

"Oh yes! Of course," Sophie stammered, the towel now covering her seeping chest region as well. "Yes, I dallied a bit with the laps but I will join you in just a moment!" With that, Sophie bounded past the gawking wiener man, or *"wanker,"* as her internal dialogue hissed against the back of her ears. *This is getting interesting.*

As Sophie made her way back to her hotel room to dry off and change into less dripping clothing, her internal dialogue was in full power. *Just because he saved you from that bizarre wanker doesn't mean he isn't one himself. I mean, the guy owns snap-on pants for heaven's sake!* Sophie silenced her inner voice. After all, it was best not to think when approaching the idea of a date. It would save her inner dialogue from having to say *I told you so* later on.

A few drinks later, Sophie found herself laughing in the company of Mr. Wild Ride, whose name turned out to be Eric Jackson. She had resorted to her best talent: getting people to tell her all about themselves. Eric's life had not been wasted. He had trained in the Air Force to be a pilot on multi-engine airplanes and had gone on to work for a major airline. He flew with the airline for a decade before realizing he wanted to fly in a different way. He'd been fascinated by the barnstormers of the post World War I days, when the Army unloaded scores of de Havilland DH-4's and old Curtiss Jennies into the hands of adventurous farm boys and some girls. He joked to Sophie that these particular airplanes were also known as "flying coffins," but when he saw her concern, he didn't elaborate. At any rate, his hobby of aviation history inspired a new route in life. He now championed the life of a small-town pilot, ferrying cargo sometimes, and offering rides to the general public over scenic vistas at other times.

Sophie gulped down the last dregs of her third beer. "Hah! Your life is a sitcom! Just like that television show where the crew flies out of Nantucket Island!"

Eric smiled. "Well, kind of, only less glamorous for me. But my life has more meaning now than it ever did flying "the bus" as I used to call it, from Tokyo to San Francisco. After a while, my life consisted of lonely hotels, catnaps in the airplane pilot's bunks because the flights were so long, and airport food. It was not a life for me."

Sophie nodded. "Kind of reminds me of *this* life," she said, pointing to the hotel bar and its occupants. She felt herself getting light headed and then remembered that she had taken her medications at dinner time.

"Uh oh," Sophie murmured, putting her hand to her head.

Eric laughed. "Is it time for you to go to sleep?"

"Yes, I think so. Please excuse me. It was nice meeting you." Sophie's voice trailed off as she took her purse off the back of her bar stool.

"Please, let me walk you back to your hotel room," Eric said, pulling her bar stool back and holding out his arm, gentleman style. *But was he a true gentleman?*

Sophie eyed him warily. "I've heard this before."

A light bulb went off behind Eric's eyes. "Oh, no, I didn't mean *that*. I very literally meant, er, can I see you safely to your hotel room door? That's all. Nothing more."

"Yeah, okay." Sophie said rather listlessly. She'd had such a lovely time. She hoped he wouldn't ruin it by making her do the oldest escape trick in the book. No—not that one! Not the one where her knee might accidentally connect with his midsection. Maybe this was the second oldest escape trick in the book. She had actually used her shoe heel on a belligerent man's toes once in order to escape his unwanted advances. But tonight, she was wearing flats. *Damn!*

As they walked down the hallway, Sophie was aware of her arm through his and his steady gait while she wobbled along. She could feel the hardness of his muscles and raised her eyebrows appreciatively. Mr. Wild Ride worked out. They reached her hotel room door.

"Here is where I must say good night," she said, trying to sound nice, but not too nice. Eric smiled and bowed slightly, backing up. But Sophie forgot to disengage her arm from his and she stumbled forward and crashed against him, who in turn, fell against the wall. Sophie giggled a bit.

"Sorry about that! I didn't pay the gravity bill this month!" And then she stole a kiss. Eric, startled, did not kiss back. Anxiety welled up in her throat. Had she gone too far? But then, his arms wrapped around her shoulders and the kiss deepened. Sophie's senses were electrified and her toes curled. She pulled away quickly and slid her hotel card into the door lock. Without a backwards glance, she closed the door behind her.

III

"Hey Susana, how is everything going?" Gabby asked as she breezed by the front office on her way to unload some groceries. She poked her head back into the office.

"Did you hear from Sophie yet?"

"Oh, yes! Sophie. She left a message while I was...occupied. She got to the convention hall and was just about to set up the booth when she called. She left her hotel phone number, should we need to reach her. Otherwise, she said she'd be back tomorrow by noontime. She had some work to do at the library tomorrow night. She mentioned something about women suffering, blah blah blah." Susana doodled a cobweb on the edge of her monthly planner desktop protector. *Perhaps a metaphor for her life?*

Gabby sauntered into the room and took a closer look at Susana's face. She was flushed and looking mighty guilty about something.

"Susana, you know that Sophie is studying woman 'suffrage'—the history of women getting the vote in this country. And yes, I suppose you could say that women 'suffered,' but that's not exactly what your older sister is basing her future hopes, dreams, and university job on." Gabby walked around closer still to Susana's desk.

"Something tells me that you had quite a diversion this afternoon." Gabby's intensely dark eyes bored into Susana, who was trying to be nonchalant—putting the finishing touches on the spider that belonged to the doodled web.

"Oh, yes, that's right, I accidentally flung a pen across the room and did some damage to the carpet. I'm terribly sorry." Susana avoided eye contact with Gabby. *Damn her. She was just too perceptive. Small wonder Sophie always lied with a smile on her face when Gabby was in the room.*

"Hmmm...I think there's more to this story," Gabby said, sitting down at the lounge chair in front of Susana's desk. "Dish, woman, dish. Don't think I didn't see Mr. Handyman coming up the walk just as I was backing out of the driveway this morning?"

Susana rolled her eyes. "Are there no secrets in this house?"

"Not while I'm around, now talk!"

"You'd make a great high school principal, you know that Gabby?"

"Don't try to smokescreen me young lady!" Gabby said wickedly.

"Okay, okay. Geesh! His name is Nathan Lake. He prefers 'Nate.' I prefer 'Yummy tool belt guy'. He's working on the house down the street and wanted to see our plumbing since our house is similar to that one. I showed him our...plumbing." Susana cursed her inability to avoid suggestive phrasing.

"Yeah, I'll just bet you did! He could probably come by whenever he wants to 'fix' things. Did you invite him to our cocktail party in a few weeks?" Gabby rose and stood at the doorway.

"Now, why on earth would I do something like that," Susana asked slyly. There was no getting anything past Gabby.

Gabby waved. "I'm headed upstairs to update our books. I've just been to the bank with some payments. Need anything before I go?"

Susana sighed. "No, no, you've already sucked all the information out of me. I've got some calls to make for reservations in Bar Harbor and a lumberjack room up in Greenville."

"Oh, the lumberjack room! My favorite!" With that, Gabby skipped up the steps, briefcase in hand. Truth be told, she was looking forward to a little private time in which to "chat" with her honey, Thad Green, who was stationed in Iraq. By "chat" she meant Instant Messaging via computer. They agreed on a time when they would both be on the Internet and could interact through text messages. The time was drawing near. She sat down briefly on her bed, holding a photograph taken of the two of them at Ellis Island. They had brought a picnic. He had proposed to her and she had accepted. He thought he was in the clear of military duty. Their life together lay before them like a river flowing in the sun. Three days later, terrorist attacks brought New York and Washington, D.C. to a standstill. Thad kept renewing his tour of duty, promising it would be his last. Gabby should have let him go, found someone else, gotten on with her life. But she couldn't. She loved Thad. He was the one. She would wait as long as it took to have a real future with him. A future that involved marriage and babies. A future that Sophie and Susana did not seem to favor.

Gabby rose and went to her laptop at her desk by the attic window. It was nice to have the privacy of an attic bedroom; no one could hear her crying herself to sleep up here. The girls didn't even know Gabby was engaged. Sophie just thought her relationship with Thad was a congenial one—a long-distance friendship, with benefits when he came back on leave. In truth, she ached for Thad and the long separations from him tore at her heart. It was almost more than she could bear at times. But she tried not to be angry. She tried to respect his decision. She tried to show him love in any way that she could.

Her laptop beeped as she turned it on. Thirty seconds later, she was logging into her email account and messaging Thad. There was a brief delay. This delay always brought on a sick taste in her mouth. For a split second she wondered if Thad would answer at all. Maybe his unit had been moved. Maybe he'd been blown up in a roadside bomb. Maybe his feelings were stretched thin. She knew in her gut though, that the latter was not the case. Their "chats" were far ranging. Some days, he was distant and she could tell that he was struggling. Other days, he was incredibly funny or romantic. And sometimes, when no was around, they attempted the next best thing to actual physical relations. It felt utterly ridiculous, but still somehow filled a need inside of her.

Today, Thad informed her, was a hard day. Someone they trusted had shot one of his buddies. The shooter got away, never to be seen again. Their chat was brief, with Gabby doing her best to console him. What could she say? She had absolutely no idea of the depth of his misery over there in the "sand box." And, bidding her lover goodbye, Gabby curled up in her bed, feeling horrible and guilty, thankful that it had been Thad's friend and not him who had been shot. Love could be more painful than anything else.

A while later, Gabby awoke. Her pillow was tear-stained. She was no longer filled with grief, but rather ponderous of this curious time in her life. She mused that perhaps she and the Hammond sisters were all brought together in a kind of way station—biding time until the real life began. For her, it was a life with Thad. For Sophie, it was an academic life—a profession she could pursue even if it was from a wheelchair. For Susana, whom Gabby was just getting to know, it was about finding herself; figuring out what her true strengths really were.

Gabby went back to her laptop. At times like this, the best thing to do was work. She clicked on their website. The site still needed "something," although no matter how long she stared at the screen, she couldn't determine what. This was Sophie's department. Gabby would be sure to pick her brain once she returned from the business expo.

Thinking about Sophie, Gabby remembered a conversation they'd once had.

"Hey, Gabby, promise me something?" Sophie had asked her when they were sitting on the steps of the university library.

"What's that?" Gabby asked, watching her friend.

"If I finally lose all of my marbles from reading too many bad history books and threaten to climb to the top of the library roof with a rifle and start picking off innocent bystanders, you'll hold me back, right?" Sophie smiled wryly, indicating that she was academically fatigued.

"Yes, yes, I promise to talk you down from the ledge," Gabby said lamely.

"But seriously, promise me that if you and Thad ever get serious, you won't leave me behind." Sophie looked straight ahead. "Say you won't desert me. You're the only one who has ever really understood me."

"You know, my friend, that I wouldn't do that," Gabby reassured her.

"Good," Sophie said and grinned at her friend. "I guess there will be no shooting today. Let's go see what Brian has cooked up for us in the cafeteria."

"Oh goody," Gabby chirped falsely, "I need my daily dose of cyanide."

Gabby snapped back to the current moment, her eyes fixated on their website. "Yes," she said aloud to herself, "It's missing…something."

IV

"We need what?" Gabby asked, inching forward in her seat on the front porch. Her red jacket contrasted against the sunshiny yellow walls of the house exterior. It was early June and Sophie's lilies of the valley were in full bloom and the air was fragrant with their smell. The proprietors of Pirate Shirt Dot Com were having their weekly staff meeting, complete with tea and cake, a company requirement. Sophie always said if there wasn't chocolate being served, than the meeting wasn't worth attending.

Sophie's lips curled with her wicked thought. She took a bite of one of Susana's chocolate chip brownies and elaborated to Gabby and Susana.

"We need a mascot," Sophie said, licking brownie crumbs off of her fingers.

"Like an animal?" Susana queried, thinking her older sister had finally gone off her rocker.

"No, not an animal. Really, Susana!"

Susana threw up her hands in mock frustration. "Well, when you say mascot, what exactly do you mean?"

"I mean that we need a man in a pirate shirt. A hot man. A really hot man!" Sophie searched her plate for any traces of extra brownie, even crumbs would suffice. God forbid she actually help herself to a second brownie!

"Well, I bet Nate, the *very* handy tool man would make a fantastic pirate. Susana, can you advise us on this one? Has he ever mentioned buried treasure?" Gabby laughed, trying not to spit out brownie.

"Yeah, she's a regular pirate's treasure, a sunken chest!" Sophie chimed in.

Susana rolled her eyes, trying to be game to her sister's "best friend's club" that consisted of Sophie and Gabby alone, and whose tactics included mocking her every move.

"Ha ha," Susana drolled sarcastically. "You're a real riot. A Quiet Riot!" There, she had righted the situation by pulling out of her brain bank a particularly bad rock music pun. That'd show them not to mess with her!

"Anyway," Sophie continued, ignoring Susana's conversational feat, "I'm thinking that we could stake out some of the local gyms for a beefcake type. You know the guy, we all do. He's the one who's shaved his chest hair and oiled up his biceps and pectoral muscles. He wears the proverbial 'wife beater' shirt—the white t-shirt with no sleeves."

"Yeah, sure, we get it, but how do we convince this beefcake to pose for our website and promotional materials?" Gabby asked.

"Odds are, if we offer him some nominal cash—I know Gabby, before you even speak, it would have to be extremely nominal—and the chance to put his perfectly sculpted image out there, our man would gladly do it. We just have to find the right guy—oh, and buy a pirate shirt that would fit him!"

"And tights! Don't forget tights!" Susana quipped.

"Yes, of course, tights! Definitely should have tights on." Sophie agreed.

"Oh my god. You two are ruining a perfectly good brownie with your pirate shirt and tights comments!" Gabby moaned, holding her head in fake pain.

"Hey, easy enough for you to say! You don't have to endure the polyester dreamboats at business expos!" Sophie cried.

"Oh, yeah, speaking of polyester dreamboats, a guy keeps calling for you, Sophie. Someone named Eric. But he doesn't sound old or pervy. Did you actually meet a normal guy? He said you'd remember him from the Nashua, New Hampshire convention." Susana looked over to Gabby conspiratoraily.

Sophie studied her friend and sister, trying to decide the best approach. It was near to impossible to get anything by Gabby and her sister knew her pretty well too. *Damn.*

"Yes, I did meet someone in Nashua, but I'm rather surprised he called." Sophie patted down her napkin. "Okay, what else is on the agenda?" She questioned smoothly.

"No way! Back the truck up!" Susana trilled.

"Yeah, you don't get to gloss over this one, Missy!" Gabby said.

"Okay, okay. His name is Eric Jackson. Sure, he seems normal and he's mildly attractive, but really, honestly, could I date someone who calls his flying business "Wild Ride Flying Lessons! No, I could not!" Sophie tried to make this remark the conclusion to this particularly uncomfortable conversation. It was hard to maintain her privacy while living with her best friend and her sister.

"Oh, I bet he does offer a wild ride!" Susana slapped her hand against the table. "Well? Did you find out?"

Sophie scoffed. "What's that supposed to mean?" Gabby chuckled.

"I mean," Susana feigned insult, "Did you take flying lessons?"

"No time." Sophie said, shrugging her shoulders. "I mean, there was no time for *anything*."

Gabby and Susana made hooting and hollering sounds. Susana put her fingers to her lips and whistled.

In mid-whistle, Nate appeared out of nowhere at their front porch steps.

"Good afternoon ladies." He glanced at their notebooks and plate of brownies at the center of the table. "Am I interrupting anything?"

Sophie stiffened and put on her professional face. "No, of course not, we were just wrapping up the end of our meeting." She rose and smoothed out her sundress. "You must be Nate." She shook his hand. Gabby followed behind her. "This is Sophie, Susana's older sister, and I'm Gabby."

"Very nice to meet you both," Nate said, his shyness betraying his able tool-belted image. "I was stopping by to see Susana, I mean, to install this copper pipe that I picked up at the hardware store last week. You have a corroded pipe under your kitchen sink and I thought it might be good to replace it."

Susana sputtered. "Oh, Nate, you didn't have to do that! You're not our personal handyman."

Nate's blue eyes flickered. "I could be your handyman for the price of one chocolate brownie." Susana stood motionless, her mortification almost complete.

Sophie briskly reached in, grabbed a plate, threw a brownie and a napkin on the plate, and held it out for Nate. "Done and done! Welcome to Pirate Shirt Dot Com! I think we could easily trade in food for your expertise," Sophie trailed off, turning around to stare at her younger sister suggestively.

Susana gave Sophie a death look. "What Sophie is trying to say is: You're hired!"

Gabby chimed in. "Yes, and you're welcome to attend any of our company events. I trust you know about the lawn party we're

SHANNON M. RISK

having this Saturday at 5 p.m.? It would be lovely if you could make it."

"Oh, yes, I think I can. Susana had given me some postcard about it a few weeks ago." Sophie and Gabby both turned to Susana and raised their eyebrows. The three women knew that was secret code for: *Wink wink. Nudge nudge. Say no more!*

Susana decided to end this callous display. "Nate, follow me." And jokingly, she picked up the plate of remaining brownies and took it with her, effectively punishing her sister and Gabby for picking on her in front of yummy tool belt guy.

V

The sounds of Bossa Nova music filtered out over the back lawn of the Pirate Shirt Dot Com headquarters. Fifty guests were clustered throughout the property, some enjoying the small gazebo Sophie had installed only days before and had hastily arranged lilies to surround it. Others were seated on the wicker furniture at the wrap-around front porch, basking in the cool early evening air and the soft light of the Chinese lanterns fastened to the trim. Many were gathered at the wet bar or following waiters carrying trays of hors d'oerves. Susana stood near the front of the house, keeping an eye on incoming traffic and acting as greeter. Really, she was looking out for her favorite handyman. Gabby was engaged in a business conversation with one of their clients who worked in banking. She snagged a treat every time the waiter walked by. And Sophie floated around, wishing her guests well and supervising the music, food and drinks. She occasionally introduced single women to single men or congratulated those celebrating anniversaries through Pirate Shirt Dot Com romantic adventure packages. The evening was going very well. Sophie crossed her arms across her chest, smiling satisfactorily.

Sophie had a big announcement to make. Well, okay, so it wasn't really all that big, but she wanted her clients to feel as though they were a part of this enterprise. She nodded to the deejay who gradually faded the Bossa Nova music.

"Ladies and gentleman, Sophie Hammond, the President of Pirate Shirt Dot Com humbly requests your attention for an announcement." People stopped their conversations and faced towards Sophie.

Clasping her hands in front of her, Sophie confidently addressed the group.

"We at Pirate Shirt Dot Com are thrilled that you were able to attend our first lawn party. We hope to have many more of these in the future." There was some polite applause. Sophie continued, "I would like to introduce the two other employees of this firm. At the front of the house, you probably met my beautiful younger sister, Susana Hammond. She is also the voice that you hear when you call us. Please give her a hand." More polite clapping followed, with guests straining to see who Susana was out of the corners of their eyes.

"I'd like to also recognize Gabby Killeen, our business manager and Webmaster, standing next to Ted Roberts." People turned and smiled at the very professional looking Gabby who nodded in every direction.

"We are gearing up to offer some new romantic adventures in the fall and I encourage you to ask any of the staff if you are interested in hearing more. Perhaps you would enjoy spelunking in the caves in the western mountains or go white water rafting at Baxter State Park. Or maybe you'd rather stay indoors at a luxury suite at Sugarloaf Mountain ski resort. We are here to make it happen for you!" Sophie smiled broadly.

"As part of our new advertising campaign, we will also recognize…" Sophie paused, catching the flash of a man's suit jacket out of the corner of her eyes. It was him. It was Eric Jackson. And man-oh-man did he look good. He had a boyish expression on his face as he stopped near the deejay table. Flustered, Sophie tried to regain composure.

"We will also recognize our new representative. We are now searching for the man who will embody Pirate Shirt Dot Com. You will see him on our website and all materials starting in the fall. So, if you know of someone you think might be suitable for this campaign, please do give us a call." Sophie watched Eric get a white wine from the bar.

Distracted, she said, "Thanks again for your support. Please enjoy the rest of the evening." More applause followed as Sophie signaled to the deejay to begin the music again. Guests turned to face each other, exclamations and laughter dotting the early evening air.

Sophie suddenly felt very awkward. She had not returned any of Eric's calls and had been very hush-hush about what happened in New Hampshire. But here he was—the man she had kissed hungrily for a few seconds, and the man on whose face she had abruptly slammed the door. One had to admire his persistence.

Eric did not give Sophie the option of escape. He sauntered over to her. "If I didn't know better, I'd say you were avoiding me."

"Oh, no," Sophie babbled, trying to find the words, "That's not it at all."

"Don't worry. I was in Bangor for business and your sister, who has been very charming and accommodating, invited me to your lawn party. She said you'd be pleased to see me. She also tried to get information out of me, but I wouldn't talk."

He was making fun of her. He was ridiculing the whole thing. Sophie didn't know what to say. How could she explain why she had slammed the hotel door in his face? Her explanation would be too heavy, and would drive him away. Better, she always reasoned, not to even encourage a relationship. That way, men wouldn't leave her when they learned the truth about her deteriorating health.

"Well, thank you for not supplying the enemy, I mean, my sister, with any good nuggets. It would all be blown out of proportion anyway." Sophie grabbed a glass of wine off a passing waiter's tray. It had always been her policy not to drink at her work events, but this was a huge exception, she thought.

"It's nice of you to stop by. Would you like a tour?" Sophie offered, at a loss of how she could show him that she meant no hard feelings.

"Sure," Eric said, smiling at her, melting her by his very presence. Why did he have to have a sculpted jaw line, dark, sultry eyes, recklessly cropped curly hair, broad shoulders and lean hips? Why did he have to be comfortably taller than she was? He must have stood at six feet four inches, which, compared to her five feet eleven inches, meant something indeed. Ask any tall woman. This was heaven.

Sophie led the way down the back yard path and up to the back porch. She opened the door that led to the kitchen. Talking back to him over her shoulder, she practiced her small talk. "When Gabby and I first looked at this house, we weren't sure we were up for all of the work it would take to bring this house up to speed. We worked feverishly for six months, launching our business by day and painting and plastering in the evenings."

"You have a lovely home. You should be proud of it. Still, there is a lot to clean in an old Victorian house like this." Eric followed closely behind her as they made their way through the kitchen and into the front foyer.

"Oh," Sophie said casually, "It's not a big deal, we split all the work pretty evenly. Susana is an outstanding cook, Gabby does the dishes, and I tend to the garden. We're a family of sorts. We alternate cleaning the bathrooms, getting groceries, vacuuming, and taking out the garbage."

"And who are these two little devils?" Eric asked, looking down at the cats, who were both curled up, back-to-back, in an antique overstuffed chair at the side of the front entrance foyer.

"Bobo and Mitzi. They are brother and sister. We got them about four months ago. Someone had the gall to drop them off at the pound. We think they're about five years old. Who would do such a thing?" Sophie asked rhetorically.

"Good question indeed." Eric stooped down to give each cat a pat on the head.

Sophie leaned down to do the same but in a repeat performance, she fell right into Eric, who caught her, and helped her stand up. Before she could apologize, he drew her into his arms and kissed her. His body was warm and calming but his lips elicited a steamy response from Sophie. She found herself quite out of breath because her heart had gone haywire. She felt as though she was floating out of her shoes. Eric pulled slightly away and looked into her eyes.

"Why didn't you call back? Am I such a bad kisser? Did I do something to offend you?" Now his deep brown eyes bored into her and there was no escape.

"No...I...you..." Sophie took a deep breath. "You are a good kisser. I'm sorry, it's just, I can't..." she looked down to her shoes. "I can't really date. I just...I just don't have the time." Realizing this was a worthy excuse, she pursued it further. "You see, I'm in graduate school and, what with my job here, I'm just too busy to..."

"Return nice men's phone calls?" Eric joked. When he saw her face, he laughed and pulled her closer. "I'm just kidding. You don't owe me anything. It's just that I thought we had a nice time back there in New Hampshire, and quite honestly, I don't meet many women like you."

"Like me?" Sophie asked.

"Well, frankly, when I go to those conventions, I usually meet elderly women, grandmother types, who want to fix me up with their sixteen-year-old granddaughters. Or I get the grandmother types who want to fix me up with themselves. And you," he looked slightly embarrassed, "You just knew so much about any history topic I brought up. And you phrased the history in a way that put my high school history teacher to shame." He stroked her hair.

"Well, yes, there are some rather dull history teachers out there, I guess. But I had three beers! *And medication—her inner dialogue whispered.* I couldn't have possibly sounded all that interesting. Besides, I live here in Bangor, and I don't even know where you live."

"I live in Farmington, about two hours from where you are. Not far, especially not in a Piper Cub airplane." He looked at her hopefully.

Sophie pulled away. "You don't want to date me. I'm complicated. I'm difficult. I'm a feminist. I don't take any crap from men." She hoped this sounded convincing enough.

"Fine, I like strong women. I like women who have goals, who have brains, and who can swim 50 laps." His last comment, meant to be a compliment, stung her. If he only knew, he'd drop her in a heartbeat. She was, after all, damaged goods. Thunderbolts did strike healthy young women from time to time.

But she was also very lonely and it felt good to have this man's attention. Would it be a crime to enjoy his company, making no promises towards the future? She liked to ride in airplanes and had a bit of experience riding in vintage airplanes. He was watching her and she was sure he could see her wrestling with her own thoughts.

"Eric, I don't know what to say. I'd like to date you, but all of my past relationships have ended. It's exhausting to start something, invest a lot of heart and time into it and then see it all disintegrate." *Just like my body is disintegrating.* But still, if he took her on, there would be a moment of truth. He would show his true colors then. Could she stomach yet another cruel rejection? Sure, she was "interesting," only as long as she was also considered "healthy."

"Why don't we just take it one date at a time? I'll admit it. I find you ravishingly beautiful. When I look at you, I feel like a complete schmuck, like I don't deserve a woman like you. But darn it, I'm a good guy and I have a lot to offer."

As Sophie and Eric negotiated this new relationship, they were oblivious to the two extra pairs of ears that were straining to hear the conversation from the kitchen.

"Crack the door just a bit more!" Susana whispered too loudly into Gabby's ear. Gabby held her finger to her lips and shook her head.

"But I want to see what they're doing!" Susana insisted.

"We'll get caught and embarrass not only ourselves, but also them. This is a fragile situation; let them get to know each other."

"Do you think she'll tell him about her illness?"

"Doubtful. Not that it's anything to be ashamed of, but she's been burned before. I don't blame her in the least if she keeps that to herself for a while," Gabby commented.

"I think she should declare it right away, to see what the guy's made of," Susana said.

"Yes, she's done that. A sort of test. But the man always fails that test. Better for them to get to know her, to see how she handles her illness, to see that she is not going to fold like a house of cards. She's one tough cookie. I don't know if I could do what she does every day in her condition," Gabby said.

"You are also a tough cookie," Susana whispered, squeezing Gabby's shoulder. "You are the brave one, with Thad over in Iraq. You never once complain about it though you have every reason to. You and my sister both are my idols." Susana laughed, "I want to grow up and be just like you!"

Gabby gave her a small shove and smiled. It was a sad smile. Her courage would not bring Thad back from the Gulf.

They pushed the kitchen door open just a bit more because the conversation had stopped. Sophie was in Eric's arms, kissing him passionately. There was a certain grace to the scene.

Gabby looked at Susana. "I hope this one doesn't hurt her. So help me, I'll..." her voice trailed off.

"I know," Susana said, "Me too."

VI

Gabby, Sophie, and Susana made their way down the pedestrian path that ran along the Kenduskaeg Stream and away from Bangor proper into the suburbs. It was Sunday morning, and since none of them were church-going people, they liked to spend their time convening with nature.

"Go over this plan again?" Susana asked, hollering over Gabby's shoulder to Sophie who had taken the lead. "And slow down by the way, geez! It's like the Bataan Death March, only, my evil sister is the task master!"

"You big baby!" Sophie shot back at her sister, picking up her pace.

Gabby yelled, "Hey, how come I always get stuck in between you two bickering biddies! It's starting to hurt my head. Now let's talk shop. Where do you want to go first to search for Mr. Pirate Shirt?"

"Well," Sophie said, "I was thinking the University has a weight room. We could go scope that out."

"In these clothes?" Susana, ever the fashionista, complained.

"Precisely in these clothes," Sophie said. "I mean, how weird would we look in business suits in a gym?"

"Still, it might be good to bring along some of our company literature to show we are not full of crap," Gabby said, "Tucked discreetly in a gym bag, of course."

"We will always be full of crap," Susana sang out in her best opera-like voice. She and Sophie had a game called "Opera Voice" where they sang snotty things to each other with as much fake vibrato as possible. It was one of the bizarre inner family traits that had survived into adulthood. The sisters were often unaware that others were around when singing opera style. One time, they freaked out a tourist family getting out of their car in a Cambridge parking garage.

"Crap!" Sophie sang, drawing out the word with a full aria.

"Aw, that's just touching," Gabby spat, assuming the lead ahead of the two sisters on the trail.

Later that day, the three women arrived at the university campus and parked their car next to the gym.

"I can't believe this, but I'm actually kind of nervous," Sophie said.

"Nonsense. Just treat it as business. We go in, we select our guy, we approach him, we pitch our idea, he accepts, hands are shaken, his name is signed in blood to this contract I so lovingly prepared, and then we're done. We own his soul forever more. Simple."

"Yeah, simple," Susana whined, getting out of the backseat. "Sophie, you do the talking. You've gotten the most action out of all of us lately." She was referring to the lip lock Sophie had engaged in only last weekend with the very sexy pilot Eric Jackson. The same pilot, rumor had it, who was slated to fly into Bangor on Friday.

Sophie shot her sister a look and took long strides towards the gym door. "Yeah, if he's not wearing a tool belt, he's definitely out of your league," she sniped at her sister.

"Oh, ha ha!" Susana yelled after her.

Once inside, the air was foggy—filled with an unidentifiable smell, a mix of competing cologne, laundry detergent, anti-bacterial spray, and sweat.

"Am I repulsed? I'm not sure," Susana whispered under her breath to no one in particular. Only, she wasn't addressing the peculiar smell, but rather the odd assortment of gym clothing.

"If you had your way, dear sister, these guys would all be dressed in coordinating "Gym Ken Doll" outfits. Very manly!" Sophie scanned the room, following Gabby's gaze to a lone muscle man in the corner doing sit-ups.

"What do you think?" Gabby asked the sisters.

"I think he's our man," Sophie said, eyeing him appreciatively. She slowly approached him, putting on her most winning smile. "The Joker" by the Steve Miller Band—always playing in manly scenarios—was blaring out of one of the gym speakers.

"Hey there, I'm Sophie." The man was getting up from his sit-ups, but did not extend his hand.

"I'm representing a local roman…dating service, and we're looking for a cover model to put on all of our advertising. You look like just the man for the job." Sophie bit her lip, preferring to be direct.

The man turned his head sideways, trying to make sense of this weird proposition. "Uh, what would I be doing for this advertising thingy?"

Sophie smiled again to reassure him. "Our company is called Pirate Shirt Dot Com, you know, it's a joke," she laughed, but quickly continued when the muscle man did not join her in laughter, "We need a man with a nice physique to be photographed in a pirate shirt and…tights…but it would be on our website, our company literature, and of course, we could pay you." She said that last part almost too quickly.

The man gave her a weird look and walked away. Sophie mouthed the word "okay" to herself and headed back, defeated, to her friends. But instead of finding them where she'd left them, they were already engaging another muscle man and it seemed that things were going well. She joined them.

"Really? Would the camera get the full scope of these babies?" He flexed his arms for emphasis.

"You bet!" Susana said, egging him on.

Sophie studied him. Well, a bit on the simple side, he was, but definitely good looking. They didn't need him to say anything after all, just to stand there and look like a handsome modern-day pirate. Where was the early-forty-ish Harrison Ford when one needed him?

Gabby had the paperwork out and was going through each part of the short contract, reviewing his pay, etc. He nodded vigorously, obviously a little intimidated by the legalese that Gabby had written. But he was up for it and that's what mattered.

"Great!" Gabby sealed the deal with a handshake. She had his phone number and he had her business card. She left him with the paperwork to review again at his leisure, but reminded him that they hoped to hold the photograph session very soon. The muscleman, whose name was Rob, had begun to flirt with Susana before Gabby and Sophie came to her rescue.

"Susana, isn't it time for your boyfriend's baseball game?"

"Oh, right! How silly of me!" Susana waved goodbye and ran after Gabby and Sophie.

Back in the car, Gabby lamented. "Why did he have to be the stereotype?"

Sophie laughed. "I think nothing but the stereotype would do!"

Susana crossed her arms, looking irritated. "He called me 'Red.' Am I going to have to endure that for the photo session?"

Sophie glanced over her shoulder as she backed out of the parking spot. "Afraid so, 'Red.'" Susana threw a stick of gum at the back of her sister's head.

VII

"So, Nate, why weren't you at our lawn party?" Susana asked, kneeling down beside Nate as he worked on the first floor front hall bathroom pipes of Pirate Shirt Dot Com.

He took his time in answering her. Susana bit her lip, realizing that perhaps she had fallen for him, and he didn't return her feelings.

"I had a family emergency," Nate said, tightening a bolt. "I wanted to come to the lawn party, really." He flashed an earnest blue-eyed smile at Susana that definitely reassured her that it wasn't a one-way street.

Sitting on the backs of his legs, Nate put down his wrench and took a deep breath.

"My mother is dying of cancer and she was very weak with pneumonia that weekend of your lawn party. Since I'm the only child who lives locally, I have spent all of my non-working hours by her side. My brother and sister actually flew in to be with her, thinking she might die. But she rebounded." Nate turned to Susana who was gripped by his sadness.

"It was actually the first time all of us have been in the same room for years. Unfortunately, we were all there because our mother is dying." He wiped his brow and cleared his throat and Susana thought he might break down on the spot. She started to move towards him to offer a comforting hug, but when he shrugged his shoulders and stood up, Susana shrank back into propriety.

"Well, we did have some good conversations and we talked a lot about dad—he died five years ago of a heart attack. Taught me everything I know about fixing stuff."

"Good man," Susana offered. "Nate, I'm so sorry about your mother. Please know that you are always welcome here, even if it's just to have some time to yourself. I'd be happy to cook you up a nice dinner anytime you want one." She smiled, trying to show her good intentions.

Nate's eyes grew misty again. "Thanks, Susana." She realized that was the first time he'd ever said her name. "You ladies are becoming my home away from home."

"Yeah, but not just because we have too many things in our house that need fixing!" Susana laughed. "We like having you here…I like having you here."

Nate studied her for a moment. "Thanks, that means a lot." Without further comment, he turned and walked out into the hallway.

"I need to get back to work. Let me know if there are any more problems with the sink."

Before he could leave, Susana called out: "Wait!" She ran back to the kitchen, opened the jar of cookies that she had baked the day before, and put a few cookies in a Tupperware container.

"Take these. They don't begin to pay you for your help, but I hope you enjoy them." She handed him the container and walked him to the door. Once he had gone, Susana leaned against the door.

"Oh boy!" She said, feeling silly about worrying about his lawn party attendance. She was reminded that life was much bigger than a party here, an event there. She walked into her office just left of the front door and sat in the desk chair. Was this her family? Her sister and Gabby? How long would this family last? Did she want something else in life? She had always fantasized about being a home decorator, but the prospect of starting out seemed scary. She didn't want to be a glorified secretary, with her older sister as "boss," for the rest of her life. Susana meant no insult to Sophie and Gabby, but she wanted something more. How to get that something more was the problem. She felt as if her feet were mired in quicksand.

It's a beautiful June day here in Bangor, Gabby wrote in a text message to Thad.

It's a beautiful June day here in Baghdad too—except that it's about 115 degrees in the shade and we have bullseyes on our backs, Thad wrote back.

I'm wearing a red lace teddy. Just thought you should know, Gabby wrote, smiling devilishly.

Really? OMG, really!

No! Not really! LOL! I don't wear a red lace teddy during the day. Our clients might get the wrong idea...

Who cares about the clients? In my world, you are always dressed a la Victoria's Secret.

Yes, okay then, the red lace teddy it is...only, I don't own one.

You will if I have anything to say about it!

Yes, yes, I can just see myself opening up your Christmas present in front of my parents.

Have you told your parents about our engagement?

I've told my mother. But I had hoped that you could talk to my Dad about it. Really? Are you turning out to be traditional?

Maybe...I reserve the right to pick and choose my traditions! But I really think my Dad would appreciate a man-to-man conversation about our engagement.

Sure, you'll say anything just to get me back stateside.

You got me there! Seriously, how are things?

Not too bad…not too bad. In fact…

In fact, what? Gabby drummed her fingernails against the computer keyboard.

Thad? Sweetie?

No response. Gabby frowned and took a deep breath. She counted back from ten. She got as far as eight and ran to turn the television on. The CNN station was advertising a new electric/gas hybrid automobile. She sat numbly on the edge of her bed, glancing from the blank computer screen where Thad's scrawl had just filled the room with joy, then to the back garden where the sun shone on some marigolds Sophie had planted, and then back to the newscast. She sucked in her breath. A television anchorwoman came on looking very serious.

"We've just gotten word that there have been a series of explosions in Baghdad, targeting outlying buildings in the American green zone. We have no reports of casualties yet. We will continue to follow this story as it develops."

Tears streamed down Gabby's face. How many times would she have to go through this anxious process? She turned to face the blank computer screen.

From downstairs, Susana's voice rang out. "Gabby, Sophie, soup's on!"

She heard Sophie's thudding footsteps as she made her way towards the kitchen. Gabby sat on her bed, defeated and alone. She feebly got up, cracked open her door, and lamely called out, "Am in the middle of something, will join you later!" She took her open laptop computer off the desk and placed it on the bed. She curled her body up beside it and continued her vigil between television and blank computer screen.

"So, guess who called," Susana teased between forkfuls of salad.

"Um, Mr. Snuffleupagus?" Sophie said sarcastically.

"Not quite—this guy's less furry than Mr. Snuffleupagus." Susana faked a swoon, her hand over her forehead.

"Eric called? I swear you are totally encouraging this. You know how busy I am. I cannot carry on a relationship with a guy who's named his business 'Wild Ride'. I just can't. And don't think I didn't notice you and Gabby spying on us during the lawn party. You two are the two most non-covert people I have ever heard snickering behind a kitchen door! Honestly!"

Susana rolled her blue eyes and stuffed her mouth full of salad so she wouldn't have to answer her to sister's assessment of her surveillance skills.

"No, seriously, Sooz, I need your opinion here. I don't want to jeopardize my studies because of some guy."

"Wait—you're seriously asking for my opinion? I thought I was only around to answer the phone and scoop kitty litter." Susana said. But Sophie's expression revealed she was not amused.

"Okay, okay. My opinion is that you are a hypocrite. Our business title is not exactly the most suave one I've ever seen. Just like you, Eric probably thought it was catchy and would garner him some business. Second—he is a keeper. He came out from Farmington, only slightly invited by your younger sister with the assurance that you had a soft spot for him. And last, he is so good looking. Do you have a paper bag over your head that blocks your vision? Half of our clients, both men and women, practically fainted when he walked in the door. I swear, he's got a bottom that's…"

"Okay, okay!" Sophie interrupted. "I get it. I won't find another like him. But I still don't want to compromise my life just to date him. Long distance relationships are very draining, and what do I get out of it in the end. Just disappointment."

"Sophie, I think you are putting up a wall here to protect yourself. Frankly, what you should be asking is what you can contribute to this relationship."

"Speaking of 'relationships,' how's your relationship moving along with the Ty Pennington look-a-like?" Sophie teased, referring to the host of the Home Makeover television show, and anxious to draw the attention away from her own romantic life. Susana's comments were a bit too accurate.

"First of all, I don't *have* a relationship with Nate. Second, he fixed our bathroom sink, so be thankful." Susana then remembered Sophie's comment. "Do you really think he looks like Ty Pennington?" Susana's eyes glazed over briefly, thinking of the very handy handyman, Nate.

Sophie gave her a soft kick under the table. "He seems very much interested in you, my dear!"

Susana rolled her eyes again. "Must be my red hair, shining like a beacon, reeling him in."

"Hey, the little Mermaid got her man. So did Anne of Green Gables. I'm not so sure about Pippi Longstockings…I suspect she has remained forever a chaste 12-year-old, or something."

Susana was not amused. "Yes, but at least they had notoriety to keep them company at night. I have Bobo and Mitzi—who, I might add, like to curl up at strategic locations on my bed, effectively paper weighting me down so I cannot seem to move in the middle of the night. I am cat furniture!"

"Better you than me!" Sophie joked. "Hey, I wonder what's keeping Gabby? Perhaps she's in the middle of the financial ruin our business account books might be. Much as the romantic image of her steeped over old leather-bound ledgers may be, I can sometimes hear her cursing the computer QuickBooks program that she really uses to crunch the numbers."

"Well, maybe she's Instant Messaging Thad again. I'll leave her a plate of food in the refrigerator and she can access it at her leisure." Susana poured her sister more water.

"Thanks, Susana," Sophie said, taking her pill case out of her purse that she had hastily put on the floor before she sat down at the table. One-by-one, she popped pills into her mouth. A white pill for the daily pain, a set of yellow ones she took once a week that told her immune system to calm down, a couple of blue pills to help ease her into sleep at night, and a host of vitamins meant to fortify her body against the damage of both disease and medications. Susana discretely watched her sister take a handful of pills and a large swig of water.

"I don't envy you, taking all of those pills—or, for that matter, getting that cold injection of that biologic every other week." Susana rubbed her arm in sympathy, knowing her sister had a needle phobia. The biologic medication came as packaged needles that had to be stored in the refrigerator, only to be taken out an hour before the injection to warm up. Once, Susana had gone with Sophie to her doctor's office where they insisted that they could show her how to do her own injections. An hour later after Sophie's shaking hand had only produced tears, the nurse gave up and told her to come in before the business day every other Friday and she would give her the shot.

"Yeah," Sophie agreed, "It's kind of a cruel joke, isn't it? Putting arthritis medication into pill bottles that require one to pinch the lid with fingers that don't always cooperate. And giving oneself a shot on the back of one's arm? Same problem. Clearly, these things were designed by people with total function in their hands. I fully understand why our older relatives would 'forget' to take their medicine. They probably couldn't get the damn pill bottles open!" She lowered her plastic weekly pill dose case back into her purse and sat back at the table.

"Susana, another fine meal. How do you manage to feed us so healthily? I think I've lost five pounds since you arrived."

"Well, you may have noticed," Susana said, lowering her voice and taking on a commercial announcer's tone, "we have secretly replaced your Ben & Jerry's Phish Food ice cream with a low-fat yogurt substitute."

"Oh no, I noticed, believe me, but I knew you had my best interests at heart, dear sister! C'mon, let's clear the table. I need to get through a couple of books tonight for class tomorrow."

Susana helped Sophie clear the table. "What are you reading about tonight?"

Sophie smiled. "The amazing drama of industrialization across the nineteenth-century Connecticut River Valley! Film at eleven!" Susana made a fake gesture by putting her finger to the bridge of her nose and pretending to push up her imaginary academic spectacles.

"Sounds absolutely delightful!"

VIII

It was Thursday morning and Sophie and her friend, Jessie, were engaged in their weekly routine of combing the local thrift stores for treasure. Because both of them were graduate students, Sophie, in history, and Jessie, in anthropology, they usually found books to be the most appealing, but every now and then, there might be a unique print of a castle or a far-off place that they wanted to travel to or a captivating antique necklace. Sophie relished these treks because she and Jessie made a nice morning of it. They started with a coffee for Jessie, and a hot cocoa for Sophie at the Bagel Stop, and then on to a store on Main Street that had great things. Jessie always joked, alluding to famous Bangor resident, horror writer Stephen King, that these shops had "Needful things"—implying that one bargained with the Devil on the price of the desired object.

Sophie was trying on a dark red scarf, Bridgett Bardot style, wrapping it around her head, putting on her sunglasses, and viewing her appearance in the small mirror, when Jessie broached the topic of her marriage. It usually took about an hour to get past small talk and onto the main topic with her friend. Jessie's brown eyes were sad; her dainty face was pale. Her dirty blond hair was unkempt and her clothing rumpled. Jessie was of medium height, but today, she seemed more diminutive in stature. It was the bearing of a troubled woman. Sophie knew Jessie wasn't happy, but her friend still managed to startle her.

"It's just that there is no passion in our marriage. I'm twenty-five years old. I'm too young to have a passion-less marriage. I feel trapped every time I walk in the door." She picked up a vase made of seashells, turning it in the light, but not really seeing it.

"I mean we've tried marriage counseling, but it gets us nowhere. We are both so stubborn about getting our own way. I think we married too young. We were barely out of college when he proposed to me. And I had all of these wild fantasies about what marriage was supposed to be. I mean, I think at that time, I could envision our perfect house, our perfect things, and maybe even a family someday. And now, well, I feel like a praying mantis. I just want to bite his head off!"

Sophie chuckled, but then her smile eased when she saw Jessie was very serious.

"I know that people say when you get married, you should expect your partner to change. But I don't know if I like these changes. He's…different. I'm different. I'm bored," she said, pointing to her heart. "I love him, but more in a sisterly way."

"Jessie, why did you two get married? Did you have doubts even back then?"

"Yes, I had doubts, of course, just like everyone else. But our parents were so proud and from the moment we announced our engagement, our families just took off with the whole idea. I don't think we could have ended it then, even if we had some inkling that we would be having problems in our immediate future. I look around our apartment sometimes and see all the wedding gifts; the appliances, the pottery, the photo frames. They have all gathered dust, just like our marriage. Only, I don't think there's a special cleaning product to take away the dust collected on our relationship." Jessie put down the vase and covered her face with her hands. "I don't know what to do!"

Sophie escorted Jessie to a more private corner of the store. "Jessie, you are a good person. You earnestly thought you could make a go of it. Ted is a nice guy; perhaps it's time to level with him. Perhaps it's time for you both to get on with your lives. If this marriage is limiting for you, odds are it is also limiting to him because, amid the strain, he cannot express his feelings the way he wants to. I hate to bring up the 'Big D'—divorce, but maybe it's time to. I hate seeing you in pain. Life is too short to torture yourself over this." Sophie squeezed Jessie's hand.

"Is it possible," Jessie gulped, "To remain married to Ted but to see other men? Really, couldn't I have an open marriage?"

"Does Ted want that too?" Sophie asked.

"No—he said if I ever cheated on our marriage that it would be too much for him to bear. He would divorce me. But, I feel so stuck. I have my degree to finish and he's got a good job at the university museum. There is no reason he should have to leave his great job and this marriage, not to mention this town. We're in a bad place and I can't find a shovel to dig us out."

"So, what do you do next?" Sophie said, guiding her friend out of the store and over to a park bench in the city square, overlooking a canal that tamed the Kenduskeag Stream as it poured into Penobscot Bay. It was quiet at this time of day and there were no people around except for the old lady who fed the pigeons.

Hearing no response and fearing that Jessie didn't have one, Sophie attempted to change the subject. "See that elderly woman? She reminds me of a book I read by the nineteenth-century reformer, Elizabeth Cady Stanton. She kind of pre-dated Virginia Woolf's idea that every woman needs a 'room of her own'. But Stanton's idea was that, no matter what life brings us, women usually spend their last days on earth in isolation. She called it the 'solitude of self'. It wasn't necessarily a lonely way to live according to Stanton. She maintained, simply, that women should be equipped, or self-reliant, for these last years. In her time, Stanton meant that women should not be helpless with finances nor should they lack legal rights. I think, for us, it means that we should be emotionally ready to fulfill ourselves. Men and children come and go. Women are always asked to sacrifice self in order to please others. It's time that we endeavored to please ourselves. I don't mean that we should go overboard—part of pleasing ourselves is loving ourselves. This means that we shouldn't pick up a three-bottles-of Merlot-a-day habit or ditch our responsibilities. It just means that we should take care of ourselves and be happy with our own company. What do you think?"

Jessie thought about it for a while, watching leaves floating in the water through the canal. "Are you saying that I should stay with the marriage; but that intimacy might be replaced by other things? I need love in my life! I'm not like you, Sophie; I cannot fill my day with meaningful, but single, activities. I would be terribly lonely."

Sophie faced her. "I have spent so many years alone and believe me, it has not been fun. But I've always felt that if a man detracted from my life instead of enriched it, then I should move on. I figure the pain of being alone is better than living with a sub-standard situation. That said, your relationship with Ted has many good things about it too."

"Sophie, can you help me?" Jessie held her arm.

"Sure, Jessie, I just want to see you happy." Sophie reassured her, putting her hand over Jessie's.

Jessie's face took on a new pallor. "What I want to ask you to do to help me isn't really what I'd call the most responsible thing."

"Okay," Sophie said uneasily.

"Could you fix me up with one of your 'romantic adventures?' I've been to your website and it all looks so wonderful."

"Sure," Sophie breathed out a sigh of relief. "What do you think Ted might enjoy? A cruise? A woodland cabin? An airplane ride? I have a friend who operates private airplane tours over the western mountains."

Jessie shook her head. "No—I meant that I wanted to meet a man, someone other than my husband." Seeing Sophie shrink back, Jessie implored her. "Sophie, please!"

Sophie's eyes filled with tears. "Jessie, you know I would do anything for you, but not this. I just cannot help you with this." She looked searchingly into her friend's eyes. "I couldn't live with myself if I encouraged you to cheat on Ted. Honestly, if you are at this stage, I think it's time to bid adieu to the marriage. It's not so bad being single. I could help you set up your own apartment, or you could stay with Gabby, Susana, and me." She looked at her hopefully.

Jessie's spirits sank. "Sure, sure, I understand, I understand." Her voice was mottled and she was now communicating like a desperate person, repeating each phrase twice. "Don't worry, don't worry," Jessie said, her eyes now distant, "I won't bring it up again." Jessie abruptly stood. "Consider this conversation done, now, on to the next shop!" She was already halfway up the hill before Sophie arose from the park bench. She smiled and waved good-bye to the older woman who was still feeding the pigeons. The woman didn't see her. Her world now only consisted of the birds.

IX

Sophie waited anxiously at the main terminal at the Bangor Airport. She watched airplanes unload and people flood through the airport reception area. Families embraced and filled the area with chatter about summer trips, gossip about relatives, cell phone calls, and inquiries as to where the bathrooms were located. And then he appeared. She saw him only a second before he spotted her and walked over to her. He wore his leather pilot jacket and a loose-fitting pair of blue jeans. His body, perfectly sculpted, and his warm brown eyes, caused Sophie's already fluttering heart to kick it up a notch.

Eric immediately took her in his arms and enveloped her in a bear hug. He was one of the few men who met her eye-to-eye, easily standing over six feet tall. Sophie took in his musky scent, relaxing a bit in his arms. Everyone around them faded into the pale as Sophie closed her eyes against his shoulder.

"I've missed you," he whispered into her ear, giving it a small kiss.

"Me too," she murmured, certain her voice did not carry to his ears. She was wrong. He released her and gave her a light kiss, which sent streams of electricity through her body. She felt her cheeks reddening.

"So," he said, looking her over, "Those aren't exactly flying clothes. But I like them just the same." Sophie had on a yellow summer cardigan that ended in three quarter sleeves just past her elbows. She wore a knee-length floral patterned skirt and heelless brown leather sandals.

"Flying clothes?" Sophie inquired.

"Yes, I'm taking you out in my airplane today," Eric said resolutely.

"Oh! I didn't know—I would have worn jeans." Sophie said.

"Yes, sorry about that, but I wanted to surprise you," Eric said. "So, are you up for it? Flying right now? I just need to submit my flight plan to the air traffic controllers, and get your identification cleared for flight. Then, they can reschedule me for a gate of departure. We can go anywhere you like—how about Bar Harbor? I could fly you around Mount Cadillac, and out over the coastal islands. Sometimes you can see whales from the airplane. It's really magnificent."

"Sold!" Sophie said. She never turned down an airplane ride. It had been about six years since she'd last flown in a two-seater. Strangely enough, she'd had on a dress that time as well. It was an academic conference in Santa Maria, California, and she'd flown over the sand dunes at Oceanside.

"Great! Let's go make the arrangements." Eric put his arm around her shoulders. "I must warn you, however, to hold onto your skirt!" He winked at her, grinning, and Sophie put her hand to her head in mock embarrassment.

"Thank goodness I'm wearing underwear!" She gasped. Eric turned to her, shocked.

"It was a joke! Geez!" Sophie laughed, leaning into him.

Sophie grinned widely as Eric pushed down on the throttle, sending the airplane into the air in seconds. She had a headset on so that she and Eric could speak more easily. He sat in the front seat, and she sat in the only other seat directly behind him.

She looked down to her lap, watching what she could only lamely identify as a "joystick" moving in synch with Eric's own "joystick" at the front. She made a point to remember to ask him what the real name of that thingy was—surely her term was just a bit too x-rated. Also, the joystick was inappropriately moving the hem of her skirt each time Eric steered the airplane in response to the wind or his artificial horizon. There was something ridiculous in all of this. It was nothing compared to her entry into the airplane just minutes ago on the tarmac. A gush of wind had made her clutch at her skirt to keep it from blowing up. Somehow, Marilyn Monroe's big moment above a steam grate in the classic movie would not be so camp in this particular situation. Eric laughed at her attempt at modesty, and helped her into the plane.

Now, they were soaring over patches of pine trees, which darkened the land in between areas of deciduous trees. Every few hundred feet, another farmstead dotted the landscape, amid the rocky foothills of the Appalachian Mountain Chain. She could make out a dark red hue to the small scrub that grew on the rocky hills—blueberry patches. As they traveled east, the Atlantic Ocean filled the horizon. Nearing the coast, only small highways, like arteries, revealed themselves in the trees. Marshlands and old summer hotels and mansions came into view, and Sophie could see the multitude of cars and trucks that parked along coastal sights. Sailboats and fishing boats spotted the water, seeming not to move at all. There were a few planes off in the clouds, which Eric monitored on his small radar system.

"I used to fly out this way all the time for clients who had winter homes in the Sugarloaf area of Western Maine. They wanted to have lobster on the shore for Sunday brunch and be back to put a log in their fireplace at the mountain lodge by evening." Sophie nodded, feeling like a dog in the back seat of a car. The glass pane of the airplane kept her, however, from hanging her head out.

"Eric, it really is amazing. I've been here so many times, but to see it from the air is magical."

"Yes, it is my favorite place," Eric said, steering the airplane towards the outlying islands and past the small resort town of Bar Harbor. "You can see some of the big rigs further out to sea," he said, motioning towards a large cruise ship coming up from Boston.

"Those poor people," Sophie laughed, "Stuck on the little boat!"

"It feels more free up here, doesn't it," Eric agreed.

"Yes," Sophie said, feeling freer than she had in a long time. From this vantage point, all of her troubles seemed so silly, such a waste of time. She felt a twinge of disappointment as Eric turned the airplane back and headed for Bangor. The joystick jostled her skirt, eliciting a cry of surprise from Sophie. Eric turned his head and grinned like a man in love.

"Nice view!" He said. Sophie tugged her skirt down, shaking her head.

"Shouldn't you be flying the airplane?"

"Oh, yes, that, thanks!" Eric said, erupting into laughter as Sophie gave him a punishing tap on the back of his head.

Back at the residence of Pirate Shirt Dot Com, Sophie and Eric sat on the porch swing off to the right of the big front stairway. They were sipping lemonade that Susana had just brought out on a tray, her face conspiratorial.

"You two behave out here! We have to appear 'respectable' to our neighbors!"

"Respectable, hunh? Our neighbors are already counting the number of times Nate has paid us a visit. I think we're pretty well scandalized already." Susana feigned shock and outrage and politely walked back into the house to give her sister some privacy.

"So, it's you, your sister, Susana, and best friend, Gabby, who live here? Anyone else?" Eric teased, looking under a pillow on his side of the porch swing.

"Well, a very dashing young fellow named Bobo and his princess, Mitzi, also live here. In fact, we are really their servants. We exist only for their pleasure. Often, my sole function in life is to be cat furniture. I am sure you will soon be enlisted by one of them." Sophie gave the ground a push so that the porch swing would move.

"Where is Gabby? I haven't seen her all evening." Eric asked.

"She's over at the local high school helping a teacher outfit a new computer classroom. She tries to volunteer over there whenever she can. I think she likes being around the kids—it brings out some motherhood component in her or something." *It helps her to forget her boyfriend is in Iraq*, Sophie's inner dialogue said.

"That's nice of her. Now—what's her story?" Eric put his lemonade down when the porch swing stopped. He turned towards her, stroking her hair.

"Gabby? Well, her family is from Massachusetts. She came up here for graduate school in business, and then decided to stay. For the past year, she has been the brains behind this whole operation, keeping our books, updating our website. In fact, we plan to have a photo shoot this week with our new 'Pirate Man,' Rob."

"Your pirate man?" Eric said, putting his hand to her lips.

"Yes, well, we decided that our business name wasn't tacky enough. We needed to make it worse by finding a Fabio-like man to grace our website and our publicity materials. We found a local gym regular to be our official pirate man." Sophie gave Eric's finger a quick kiss. "He's so perfectly stereotypical of all of those horrid romance novels. We've found the ideal pirate shirt with all of those really terrible ruffles. I'm actually looking forward to how this will turn out. Gabby has decided that we will photograph our pirate man, I mean, Rob, in our backyard. She has a photographer friend coming in from Massachusetts. Should be a real riot!"

"Sounds like you know what you're doing," Eric teased, taking a sip from his glass of lemonade. Crickets were now chirping in the twilight air.

"I look at it more as trying to make the concept of dating fun again. We've become so weighed down by all the relationship tragedies. I think people need to be reminded that life is for living."

"What about you? Sophie, do you have any great relationship tragedies?"

"More than I care to recount, I'm afraid," Sophie sighed feeling a sudden chill in the air.

"No need to relive those experiences. Just tell me what I can do right. I hope to see more of you, Sophie." Eric's voice had grown soft.

"Oh, Eric, I don't know if I'm really the woman for you." Sophie said, pensively feeling the great moment yet to come.

"Sophie, as I told you before, I love that you are an independent person."

"Yes, I am an independent person." Sophie said darkly. "But for how long, I'm not really sure."

Eric said nothing, waiting patiently for her to continue.

"I have an illness for which there is no cure. I will rely on medication and hospitals for probably the remainder of my life."

"Sophie, what is your illness?"

She felt tears forming, seemingly behind her eyes, creating a pressure in her head. Here was the moment that he would flee, deeming her unworthy of knowing.

"I developed rheumatoid arthritis five years ago. It is genetic, although no one in my family for four generations has ever shown symptoms."

"What exactly does this mean?" Eric said quietly, trying to soothe her.

"There is no cure. Doctors aren't exactly sure what causes the immune system to go into overdrive and dispatch immune cells to attack joint tissue and then, ultimately, bones. All they can do is trick or suppress the immune system. I take pills that dull my immune system, leaving me open to all kinds of strange infections. For instance, I cannot wear earrings anymore. I have a weird cell mass that lives in my gall bladder. Most days, I battle fatigue. Some days, it's pretty bad. I feel like the walking dead." Sophie wiped away tears, surprised at her emotions. She'd thought that she had fortified herself against all of this. But speaking of it in front of Eric made her feel vulnerable.

Eric took her into his arms. "Sophie, I am so sorry."

Sophie looked into his russet eyes. There was no look of betrayal there, only concern.

"I am lucky right now. The medications are steeling me against the disease, for the most part. My feet…there is damage there. The drugs don't reach my feet. The painkiller that I take daily doesn't always mask the pain. The pain is there to remind me that the drugs aren't fully working. That my body is being dismantled—regardless. Imagine being an athletic and healthy person one day, and unable to get out of bed or even brush your teeth the next."

Sophie continued, "If I let my guard down for even a moment, my body is sluggish. I cannot relax…I cannot stop…I cannot have peace." Sophie's wet tears ingrained in Eric's shirt. "And somehow, I cannot completely trust any happiness that comes into my life. Past relationships have underlined that fact."

"Well, Sophie, I'm not going anywhere. Except, of course, back to work tomorrow morning. That is only a geographical separation. I am still with you. I am not running away."

"How can you not want to run away? I could be a huge liability. My medical bills could multiply if the disease gets out of control. I could lose the energy that I have now. I could lose everything."

"You don't truly believe that, do you Sophie? I've seen how you operate here. You are relentless in your organization and your ambition. Susana tells me there are very few failures for you in life. I believe she even said that you turn failures into gold."

"It's hard, wearying, to keep up this façade. Some days, I am so, so tired. My spirit is gone. I wonder what it would be like not to suffer any more."

"Sophie, don't talk like that. There are plenty of joys to be had in life."

She nodded in the dark, hearing him, but off in a distant place.

"Aside from past rejections," She paused, "I wonder if it's even right to have a relationship with someone. It's not fair to him either."

"You should leave that up to the guy. Sophie, you are an extraordinary person. You have no idea of how special you are. Your sister, your friend, and you are amazing. A guy with true feelings for you will stay by your side. Men who flee at the news of your illness are doing you a big favor." He kissed her forehead. Sophie flinched.

Facing him, Sophie's expression was still distant.

"Eric, I am not sure about this."

"Not sure about what? About us? Why not?"

"Because, I don't really see you pushing me around in a wheelchair in our golden years and spoon feeding me applesauce."

"Aren't you jumping the gun? There's a great chance you will live out your life just like anyone else."

"No, I don't think I am. I would rather a stranger had to endure my crippled existence than someone I loved."

"Sophie, that's not fair to the people who love you."

She shivered, pulling away from Eric.

"Life isn't fair, is it?" Sophie leapt up and ran into the house, slamming the screen door behind her. This was the second time she forced Eric out of her life.

Eric sat on the porch swing, stunned. He was insulted that she was so ready to make decisions for him, but empathetic of her dilemma. Perhaps she needed time. And too, the logic worked in reverse. He was a good man. If she didn't appreciate him, perhaps it was best for both of them to be apart.

Susana slowly opened the front screen door.

"Eric? I heard Sophie run up the stairs and slam her bedroom door. I know not to bother Sophie when she is upset. Time is the best healer for her. But is there anything I can do here?"

"Yes, thank you Susana. I need a ride to the airport." Eric got up and brushed himself off, as if the bad feelings could dissipate so easily.

X

Sophie knelt at the edge of her bed and looked out of the window at her garden. Sunlight filtered over perennials, making everything seem pristine, normal. But things weren't normal. Eric had gone back to Farmington prematurely, and it was she who had rejected him. *A pre-emptive strike.* Her inner dialogue said. *He would have eventually left me.*

There was a knock at the door. It was Gabby. She came into Sophie's bedroom and sat next to her at the edge of the bed.

"Sophie, can I talk to you about something?"

"Sure, but we don't have much time before Rob and your photographer friend show up."

"I know. This won't take long." Gabby watched Sophie get up and wobble a bit on her feet. It was a familiar sight to the household occupants. The first thirty seconds after Sophie arose from bed, she walked on the sides of her feet, her footpads were too tender until her blood started to circulate. Gabby steeled herself against any feelings of pity for her friend for the moment.

"I heard about what happened with Eric last night," Gabby said quietly.

"Oh yeah?" Sophie said, her back turned to Gabby and she raked through her closet, searching for the right outfit for the morning's photography shoot.

"Not the best move for you, Sophie," Gabby continued.

Sophie stopped sliding closet hangers and froze, her back still turned to Gabby. She said nothing.

"Will you drive off Susana and me too so that you won't have to face the improbable prospect that we'll reject you if you become ill?"

Sophie chuckled. "Yeah, I might have to!" She attempted a laugh. Gabby had been intense for the past week.

"Shame on you!" Gabby spat out.

"What?" Sophie whirled around to face her friend.

"I said shame on you! Here you have a genuine man, in full blood, offering himself up to you and you drive him away. You're not as smart as I thought you were! I looked up to you, and it turns out you are a cold, cold person."

"Excuse me! I think I have every right to make my own life decisions, thank you very much," Sophie fumed.

"You naive fool. While my fiancé is lost in the sand somewhere, you are creating a false drama. You are selfish! You sit up here obsessing about either your dissertation, the next weekend convention, your illness, or that pilot you're so willing to throw away and you never once asked me how things are going." Gabby took a deep breath, finally able to release her frustrations with her friend.

"Last night, I was crying myself to sleep for the 365th time this year, and I realized something. I realized that neither you nor Susana ever once asked me how Thad is. You never once mentioned the war. You skip around, pretending all is well with the world. You cannot pretend that these major things aren't going on in the world. Also, you take me for granted, and you don't show any concern for me. Here you are asking me to feel sorry for you! All I see is a woman who has triumphed over a disease by sheer will and modern science, and yet you fret over things that *might* happen some day. But not today! Damn it, not today!" Gabby shook with anger.

Sophie, shaken out of her stupor, dropped her shoulders and sat down by her best friend. Then she began to sob, her chest heaving violently.

"I am so sorry, Gabby. I am so sorry! I am a terrible friend. Oh my gosh, I am unbelievably negligent. I am a selfish jerk!"

Sophie slowed down her breathing and swiped at her eyes. She turned to face Gabby who had softened considerably.

"Gabby, the reason Susana and I don't mention Iraq is twofold. We figured that if we didn't mention it, we wouldn't upset you. But also, you know how we feel about the war. We decided, foolishly as I see now, that we would try to create a calming home atmosphere for you. If Susana made wholesome meals and I tended to the garden, we thought that it would help you somehow. We also thought that you might favor your privacy about the whole thing. We thought wrong. It is so clear to me now. How would I feel if no one asked me about my life!" Sophie shook her head, taking her friend's hand in hers. Then, a realization washed over her.

"Wait—Did you say *fiancé?*"

Gabby's brow furrowed. "Yes. We are engaged. We have been engaged since he visited me during his leave, and our graduation for our Master's degrees."

Sophie put her free hand to her mouth. "Oh Gabby, congratulations! Why didn't you say anything to us? I'm happy for you, and I know Susana would feel the same way."

The door opened and Susana spilled in, unable to maintain her balance with her ear pressed against the door any longer.

"Ah, the super sleuth has arrived," Sophie muttered amusedly under her breath.

"Excuse me," Susana said, not at all embarrassed, "what would I feel the same way about?" She sat down next to Sophie on the bed.

Sophie began to speak in her take-charge way, but then realized this was not her moment.

"Thad and I are engaged," Gabby said softly, proudly.

Susana smiled, "That's what I thought I'd heard out in the hall. Terrific news! Heck, I might even have to bake one of my famous devil's food cakes for this occasion."

"Well, I wouldn't celebrate so soon, Susana." Gabby said, biting her lower lip. "There have been a series of explosions around the United States green zones in Baghdad."

Sophie and Susana nodded gravely, acknowledging they'd heard the news.

"I haven't heard from Thad in a week. I casually emailed his mother, but she mentioned nothing in her terse response. I know I should have asked her if she'd heard from Thad, but what if she said she hadn't? Then it might be true. Thad might be dead." Her voice trailed off.

"Oh Gabby, I had no idea!" Sophie exclaimed, drawing her friend into her arms. "Gabby, I am so sorry. What can we do?"

Gabby cried quietly, a rare expression of sadness. "I don't know what to do. I am so confused."

Sophie straightened up a bit, ready to act. "Okay, Gabby, with your permission, I'm going to see what I can find out. Meanwhile, we have a photo shoot happening in a little while. Do you want me to reschedule it?"

"No, no, let's go forward with it. I really need the distraction."

Susana spoke up. "Fine, Gabby and I will work with the photographer and Rob while Sophie will see what she can find out about Thad. Is that a plan, Ladies?"

"Yes," the other two said in unison.

"Great," Susana bounded up from the bed, "Sophie, first things first. You stink. I think a shower is in order. Once you are squeaky clean, you can engage in whatever devious methods you will employ."

Sophie, acting innocent, said, "Why, Susana, whatever do you mean?" She wiped away a residual tear and winked at Gabby. "Don't worry, I'll find out what's happened to him."

Gabby smiled wistfully. "I know you will. You are relentless. And once we get to the bottom of this, we'll tackle your pilot."

Sophie dropped her head for the briefest of moments. "Sure, we'll do that."

"Tea? Coffee? Cakes?" Susana offered to Rob, Estrella, the photographer, and Gabby. Rob thundered over to her and filled his hands with the delicate little cakes that Susana had perfected over the winter months in the tiny studio apartment she formerly occupied. When she hearkened back to that little gas stove in that apartment, she shuddered. *The horror, the horror!* But now, the bigger horror lay in front of her.

"Delicious!" Rob declared, his mouth half full of cake. Estrella looked up from her array of equipment that she had spread all over a table. The edges of her mouth curved as she watched him.

"Where'd you find this guy," Estrella whispered to Gabby.

"Trust me, you don't want to know!" Gabby said covertly. Estrella bowed her head to hide a snicker.

"So," Rob said, in full male peacock mode, "Where do you want me to stand?"

Estrella pointed towards the gazebo. "Let's try a few shots over at the gazebo and take advantage of the late morning sun."

Rob strutted over to the gazebo, but not before grinning at Susana who tried her best to be civil to the brute.

Susana sighed and pulled out the pirate shirt. She held it up and walked across the back yard, hands outstretched, as if allowing the shirt to touch her body would pollute her good fashion sense. Rob smiled appreciatively, flexing his arms as he slid them into the sleeves. Susana folded her arms, shaking her head at his audacity.

Estrella relieved Susana by posing Rob for the best shot. Gabby observed the spectacle in the distance, relieved to find that life still offered plenty of humor. She wasn't, however, the only observer. Behind her stood Nate, who had come around to the back yard after knocking on the front door, and receiving no response. He remained partly concealed by the butterfly bushes, watching the scene.

"Susana, could you arrange Rob's sleeves so that they hang more off his shoulders? Make sure his chest is exposed in the sunlight." Nate watched Susana run up to Rob and quickly pull his sleeves down, her hands grazing his muscled torso. His breath caught in his throat at the sight. Susana continued to hover as Estrella asked her to make alterations to the billowing and ridiculous shirt on the impossibly buff man. Nate couldn't watch any longer. He stormed off, crashing into the butterfly bushes as he left.

Nate's exit drew the attention of Susana, who saw the flash of his tool belt as he swiftly fought his entanglement in the bush. She paused, reflecting on what set him off. It didn't take long to figure it out. *Oh great. Yummy tool belt guy thinks I'm fawning over this hunk of burnin' love.* Susana set her jaw, and resumed assisting Estrella in her job. She'd have to hunt Nate down later. *Hunt him down? Why—because of his jealousy?* No, she wouldn't run after him as a desperate woman. She smiled secretly—she had a plan. Of course, Rob thought she was smiling at him.

Sophie cradled the phone in her ear, waiting for her call to be put through. She picked up a pen and a pad of paper,

"Hello?" A male voice answered.

"Hi, Cameron, it's Sophie. Remember when I helped you study for that history test, you said you 'owed me one'?"

"Sophie Hammond! Of course. What can I do for you?"

"My best friend's fiancé is over in Iraq. Any chance you can access records, and find out where he is right now? She hasn't heard from him in a week and she's getting worried."

"Yeah, sure, but we never had this conversation."

"Of course! In fact, I'll pretend I never knew you!" Sophie drummed her fingers on the desk, remembering Cameron's inability to remember historical facts. Within a few minutes, Cameron had some details for her.

"Great," Sophie said, "My friend will be glad for this information. Thanks again."

As she hung up the phone, Sophie walked over to a window facing the back yard. She watched her petite friend, laughing in the sunlight, for the moment innocent of the knowledge that Sophie now had to share. She hesitated for a few moments, wanting to protect her friend for as long as she could.

XI

Susana removed the cookie sheet from the oven, releasing cinnamon fragrance into the world. Her targeted audience was not far away, in fact, just down the street. Not before long, there came a rapping at the back door beside the kitchen window.

In stepped Nate, wearing a mask of ambivalence, as if neither Susana nor her cooking had any effect on him. Yet, here he was. The two looked at each other without words.

Their studied silence was interrupted by the shrill tones of Sophie, who burst into the kitchen in her best and worst opera voice. "Susana! Your cookies are like a lu-vahhhh!"

Then she saw Susana and Nate. "Uh-oh." She slowly backed out, bowing and blowing kisses.

"And all this time, I thought you were the fun one. Turns out it was your sister." Susana glared at him.

"Have a cookie, Nate!"

"Don't you want to sing that to me?"

"Not especially."

Susana turned her back to Nate and stood by the stove. "Don't you have something to say to me?"

Nate pretended not to understand. "I don't think so."

Susana whirled around. "I saw you, hiding out in the bushes when we were photographing Rob. Let's just say your exit left little to be desired."

"Okay, fine, I was there. I cannot believe you think that his image will better sell your...merchandise."

"First of all, what right do you have to judge? I don't step in and run your business. Also, you and I are not dating. You have no reason to be jealous, especially not of that meathead. Now, have a cookie."

"I don't want a cookie."

"Yes, you do! Now eat!

Nate quickly took a cookie and bit in, crunching awkwardly.

"When you don't have anything, religion is everything." Susana said, giggling to herself.

"What?" Nate said through his sugarcoated teeth.

"Here we are in God's basement!" Susana burst out in full laughter.

"I don't follow..." Nate said, quickly taking another cookie so as not to upset the lady of the kitchen.

"Oh, I'm just repeating some phrases my ancient Grandmother used to say. But for me, they have always had a certain twist. You may have noticed that none of us in this house are particularly religious. But for me," she took a bite of a cookie, "This is heaven." She leaned back against the stove.

"These cinnamon spice cookies were the only thing my grandmother left me—and she did not realize that she did. I mean, she really thought we were all going to hell. She always made a specific point to tell me my hair was shaggy or that my thighs were too large. One day, when she was out with my Mother for a doctor's appointment, I pulled this recipe out of her Bible, quickly copied it down, and said nothing after that."

Susana continued. "She used to say that we were living in God's basement. It was her way of saying that we were living in sin, I guess, but that there was still hope for us!" She continued laughing, chewing the cookie.

Nate joined her by the stove, standing closer than a mere friend. "Susana, I have to tell you something."

Susana munched on a second cookie silently, waiting for him to continue.

"I have selfishly been showing up to fix things around here since the first day I met you." Nate looked quickly down, afraid to make eye contact.

"I know." Susana nudged Nate, who still could not bring himself to look at her.

She rolled her eyes, taking pity on his sudden shyness. "You know I have no interest in that pirate. I could never see past your shiny tool belt."

Nate looked up at her to see if she was mocking him. She met his gaze with shining blue eyes, copper-fired hair, and rosy cheeks.

He took her face in his hands, leaned in, and kissed her.

Sophie bounded up the stairs past the second floor en route to the attic. She knocked softly at Gabby's door.

"Come in." Gabby was seated at her desk, writing a letter by hand on paper to Thaddeus Green, United States Marines.

She looked up from her writing. "I'm teasing him about being over in Iraq all this time just raising camels."

Sophie sat down on Gabby's bed. "Well, do you want to hear the news?"

Gabby turned her chair around to face Sophie. Her lips tightened as she steeled herself against all the bad possibilities of her fiancé's fate.

Sophie spoke steadily. "I called an old friend of mine from graduate school who now works at the Office of the Secretary of State. He tracked down Thad's whereabouts." She paused; making sure her friend was ready. "Thad was injured in one of the recent Baghdad bombings."

Gabby's hand flew to her mouth, fearing the worst.

"He is still alive, but his injuries are such, though he couldn't ascertain what they were from the basic report he accessed, that he will be coming home. Oh Gabby, he's coming home."

Gabby's shoulders heaved as she openly wept. Sophie seated herself at Gabby's feet. She raised a handkerchief embroidered with her Mother's initials to Gabby's tear-stained face. Gabby looked to Sophie, questioning.

"Is he really coming home?"

"Yes, Gabby, he is."

"Oh! But he has been hurt. I am so grateful that he is not dead—I couldn't bear it. But I must get to him, must see him and help him through his injuries!"

"My friend said he was in an undisclosed hospital. He suspects Thad's parents will be contacted first. You should call his Mother and talk about this."

"I—I can't!"

"Yes, sure you can. I'll help you." Sophie reached for the telephone.

Three women swung on the porch swing at Pirate Shirt Dot Com. It was evening, at the end of a very long day. The crickets serenaded them, privy to all of their day's concerns. A plate of cinnamon cookies was perched on the thick porch front piece.

"So, I spoke with Mrs. Green. She had not yet heard the news that Thad was coming home. Turns out, she was just as anxious as I was. Why would I doubt that? She gave birth to him and raised him after all. I cannot explain how much I internalized my fear and grief. I was afraid to speak of it to anyone. It burrowed deep inside me, robbing me of daylight even when the sun shone down on me."

Susana rocked the swing thoughtfully. "Gabby, let me say again how sorry I am that I didn't attempt to break down that wall of grief. We're a family here. That's what we're supposed to do—butt into each other's business!"

"Yeah," Sophie nudged Gabby from the other side of the swing. "We're here to make your life uncomfortable. We were severely misguided before. From now on, we'll be extremely pushy broads."

"Fantastic!" Gabby laughed, nervously, still apprehensive about Thad's injuries.

"And what about you, dear little sister? I trust these cookies worked their magic?"

"Don't you wish you knew?" Susana taunted them, pretending that she would not reveal the afternoon's events. Sophie knew better.

"Oh, I see, so that wasn't Nate that I saw in the kitchen with you today, looking all uncomfortable?"

Susana grinned. "He did look uncomfortable, didn't he!"?

"Yessss…" Sophie said, indicating that she wanted gossip.

"Okay, so we kissed." The women swooned and almost tipped over the porch swing.

"Stop it!" Susana giggled.

"And?" Gabby and Sophie said in unison.

"And it was very nice." Susana looked down, trying to bottle her emotions.

"Nice!" Gabby said.

"Yeah, nice!" Sophie said. "But notice one and all, I didn't remain behind the kitchen door snooping on your little love affair. I gave you all the privacy in the world. Unlike two others in this house who get some kind of kick out of seeing Mr. Wild Ride and me locking lips. I won't mention any names…"

"So, welcome to the land of no privacy. Check your bags at the door so we can riffle through them!" Gabby said very professionally.

"Amen!" Susana said giving the ground another kick and setting the porch swing in motion again.

XII

"Good morning, Pirate Shirt Dot Com," Susana said enthusiastically. "Yes, we still have openings for our summer twilight cruise at Penobscot Bay in Searsport." She listened to directions on the other end of the phone.

"Right, I'll put you down, Ms. Tabor. And you can mail payment in or pay at the door."

"Yes, yes, there will be plenty of single men on board. This is a singles mixer. There will be drinks at the bar, a buffet dinner, and dancing. Dress is business casual, but bear in mind it will be windy. You don't want to wear a dress that might blow up in the wind. I had that happen to me once. It was awful. I was going down the stairs and…" The caller interrupted.

"Okay, yes, I understand. Thank you for calling, and we look forward to seeing you on the cruise."

Gabby breezed by, stopping to tug at Susana's pen. "Hey there, Estrella says she can get us some prints taken from last Saturday pretty quickly. She'll Federal Express them up from Boston tomorrow. She says we'll be very pleased with how they turned out. Especially you!"

Susana yanked her pen back. "I beg your pardon? Don't go creating love triangles where they don't exist! I am very much interested in yummy tool belt guy—not bizarre steroid pirate guy."

Gabby chuckled and, walking away, muttered, "Ah, young love."

Susana leaned over her desk and yelled after Gabby, "It is *not* young love!"

Sophie entered the house through the front door and walked into Susana's office. She had on a sports bra and some shorts; her mini walkman strapped to her arm.

"Hey Sophie, how was your run?"

"Good—I saw Nate headed this way. Should I turn the sprinkler system on now?"

"Very funny, Ms. Crazy Running Amazon, but we don't *have* a sprinkler system. I swear, between you and Gabby, you'd think I was fifteen and Nate was taking me to the prom or something."

"You're right, he's probably just here to fix something. Perhaps somebody, I mean, something has sprung a leak." Sophie quieted down with the knock at the door.

"Come in!" Susana yelled.

Sophie whispered across the desk. "So now you don't even get up to answer the door when he visits? Pretty cheeky."

Susana batted at Sophie's arm with her pen, hoping for another accidental tattooing incident, but she had no such luck.

Nate appeared in the office entryway.

"Nate, save me from this horrible little red-headed forest nymph." Sophie snarled at her sister.

"Au contraire, it is I who am being harassed by this towering giantess—back off! I have called in the National Guard!"

Sophie beat her chest, and then jokingly lifted up her arm and blew armpit air over at her sister. She then nodded to Nate and jogged up the stairs.

Susana looked menacingly up the stairs at her sister's disappearing legs for a moment and then turned, her attitude suddenly brightening, towards Nate.

"And what can I do for you, young man?"

Nate struggled for a moment, wanting to say something sarcastic, but he settled for, "You tell me."

"Is this visit business or pleasure," Susana said, playing coy.

"Pleasure, I hope." Nate came around the desk and lifted her up from her chair. "I was hoping to ask you out to dinner one of these fine nights. You're always sending me off with some delectable food in Tupperware containers, I thought I'd return the favor; only, you really don't want me to cook for you. I'm afraid you'd have to get vaccinated first."

Susana beamed. "I would be delighted to have dinner with you some night soon." Her lips found his and lingered there for quite a long time. Then the doorbell rang.

From out of nowhere, Gabby came ripping down the stairs. "I've got it!" she yelled breathlessly as her stocking feet slid across the tiled floor in the front hallway. Before she opened the front door, she collected herself.

Standing in front of Gabby on the other end was Thad.

"Thad!" She yelled, rushing into his arms. She noticed nothing around her. At this moment the world consisted only of him. When she pulled back to get a good look at him, she finally noticed the crutch under his left arm. She looked down to his foot, encased by a cast.

"Come in, come in," She said, ushering him through the doorway. She led him to the right, into the front living room. Susana and Nate watched the couple from across the hall. Nate looked at Susana who put her finger to her lips.

"Give them some time. He's back from the war. Come, we can make them some refreshments in the kitchen."

Back in the front living room, Gabby studied Thad's face. There was something wrong. "Thad, welcome home. I have missed you so much. Since we were cut off in Instant Messaging, I was panicked. Sophie called a friend at the Secretary of State's Office who said you'd been injured in the Baghdad blasts, but we didn't know where you were. They flew you home so quickly."

Thad, sounding far away, said, "Yeah, well, my injury was pretty straightforward."

"But if they flew you home, does that mean you're here to stay?" Gabby asked eagerly.

"Yes, sweetie, I'm here to stay."

Gabby wrapped her arms around Thad again, expressing her joy.

"But Gabby, there's something I need to tell you."

She sat back, bracing herself. *How bad could it be?* She reasoned.

Thad looked down at his cast. "This," he said, pointing to the cast, "is hollow."

"What?" Gabby said, not quite comprehending.

"My foot and ankle are gone, Gabby." Thad waited for her to soak it in.

A while later, Susana entered the living room, tray balanced on her arm, with Nate in tow.

"Hi Thad! Welcome back! We're so glad you're here! I brought some refreshments—some black tea and some tea cakes."

Thad, looking strangely at a white-faced Gabby, obliged Susana by taking a cake.

"Where are my manners? Thad, this is Nate. Nathan Lake. He's working on the house down the street. And Nate, this is Thad, Gabby's fiancé." The two men shook hands cordially.

"But we're obviously interrupting your conversation," Susana said, pulling away, "So, we'll just leave you with the tray. Again,

Thad, it's great to see you." She and Nate quietly left the room. There would be no eavesdropping this time. Susana looked back at Nate as they walked down the hall to the kitchen.

"They did not look like a happy couple reunited, did they?"

"No—they did not."

Back in the living room, Gabby sat back against the sofa.

"The foot is completely gone?" Thad nodded.

"But why did they put a cast on it?" Gabby asked.

"Because I didn't want my Mom to know about it yet. She's pretty emotionally fragile right now. I just couldn't let her see that. Gabby, she used to drive me to all of my track meets back in school. She'd be crushed if she knew that I can't run anymore."

Gabby stared at the cast, unbelieving.

Thad took her hand. "Gabby—there's something else I wanted to say to you today."

Gabby shook her head. "Okay, anything."

"I'm here to give you an out. If you want to break off our engagement, I won't hold it against you. I'd understand completely. I'm damaged goods. You want a husband who can be active with your children; a husband who can provide with a good job. I'm facing months of rehabilitation right now. I've been assigned to a veteran's hospital in Boston. I'll have to stay there until I recuperate. I'm not sure," he said, gritting his teeth against the sudden surge of emotion he felt, "I'm not sure what success I'll have with a prosthetic lower leg and foot."

Gabby's disbelief soon faded. Gulping back tears, she squeezed Thad's hand and then kissed him. "I'm not going anywhere. I'm not running away from this. I love you with all of my heart and I will be by your side no matter what life throws at us." Shaking with tears, she continued. "You are *not* damaged goods! This, this loss of your foot is not the end of your life. You can work through this and I will be by your side."

Thad took her into his arms as she cried. "Shhhh. It's okay. I was hoping to God you would say that, but I didn't want to pressure you. I didn't want you to feel trapped in any way. I love you so much." He looked into her eyes. "The truth is, I need you Gabby, desperately. I need your love to get me through this. I am so…angry. I know I shouldn't be. I should be thankful that I am alive, that I'm here with you. But, I feel so frustrated without my foot. And, at night, when I try to sleep, I almost go mad from the throbbing in my leg and this strange, itchy kind of feeling that my foot is still there. I forget when I need to go to the bathroom at night. I land too heavily on my left leg and end up on the floor in agony. Last night, my Mom had to help me go to the bathroom. My Mom saw me cry. Gabby, this is unchartered ground for me, right now. Everything seems so crazy and out of control."

"I know, but we'll get through this. You can yell and scream anytime you want. I won't leave your side. To me, you are a hero."

Thad quickly wiped away a tear leaking out of his nose. "Marines aren't supposed to cry," he joked. "During this last tour of duty," he said, fumbling at the inside pocket of his jacket, "I found something for you." He held out a small velvet bag.

Gabby gasped, slowly taking the bag from Thad. Opening it, she found a stunning ring sporting a large ruby and small opals surrounding it. "Thad, is this?" Gabby asked, unable to continue.

"Yes, Gabby. I never gave you a ring before to solidify our engagement. So, I'm asking again—be my wife?" Thad said, his nose fully running now beyond his will. He took out a handkerchief, held it briefly to his nose, and waited for her response.

Gabby looked at the magnificent ring. She could not find the words to express all of the emotions running through her.

"Y-yes, oh Thad, yes!" She said throwing her arms around him again.

Beaming, Thad took the ring and put it on her left hand. "Lovely," he said, looking into her eyes.

XIII

Sophie held down the vinyl tablecloth while Susana clipped it to the table. The sisters then began laying out silverware and dishes. White napkins fluttered in the late afternoon sun.

"Alright, I wonder whose veggie burger this is!" Nate called out from his station at the barbeque. Susana wrinkled her nose. "Are you making fun of my veggie burger?" She ran off to give him a poke in the arm.

"I would do nothing of the sort!" Nate said, defending himself. "I'm just curious to know how they pack grass into such a perfectly rounded little patty." Susana pretended to punch Nate who wrapped his arms around her and wrestled her into mock submission. Susana pointed to the lone veggie burger. "You treat it right!" She said, cautioning him that her "food" was to have special attention.

Gabby and Thad sat at the gazebo, watching the antics of their friends.

"Have you told them?" Thad asked.

"Well, they couldn't miss the huge rock of my finger, so they know about the imminent wedding—which Susana has begged to help me plan. But I haven't yet mentioned what's under your cast."

"You mean, what's not under my cast." Thad said softly.

Gabby smiled at him reassuringly. "We can tell them when the time is right. There is no rush here. And they won't judge you. Believe me. See Sophie there? She's been suffering from severe rheumatoid arthritis now for the past five years. In fact, someday, it might be useful for you to talk to her; compare strategies. She's been going out every morning this summer and jogging for forty-five minutes. I get tired just at the sight of her." Gabby looked back at Thad; "Anyway, we'll do everything on your watch and no one else's, okay?"

"Okay. I'm so lucky to have you Gabby." Thad kissed her sweetly at first, and then, when he was sure the others weren't watching, gave her a more passionate kiss.

Sophie finished dressing the table as Susana and Nate took care of the veggie skewers, corn-on-the-cob, hot dogs and hamburgers. She had grown silent, observing the easy manner of the two couples in her company. She felt a nagging sensation, like she could share in this happiness. It was up to her, she knew that. She had run him off—he hadn't deserted her. If she wanted him back, would he still want her? A man like Eric would surely have other women in his life. Who was she to just assume he would be home every night, waiting by the phone? Susana's giggles interrupted her thoughts. *Good, at least my little sister is happy.* Sophie looked over to the gazebo where Gabby and Thad were alternately kissing, hugging, holding hands, and generally basking in the glow of each other's presence. *What was she so afraid of? Eric was exactly the kind of guy she had hoped for all of these years. Why was she punishing him for the faults of old boyfriends? What the hell was she waiting for?*

Susana's not so subtle dinner call brought everyone to the table. For the next hour and a half, the group chattered away about Monty Python, college life, the military, and Gabby's ring. As the sun set, the men went inside to do dishes and Susana and Sophie cleaned up out back.

It started out innocently enough. One sister started singing lightly, "Oklahoma where the wind comes sweeping down the plain."

And then the other, a bit louder continued, "Where the waving wheat can sure smell sweet when the wind comes right behind the rain!"

Suddenly, both sisters stood with their hands to their hearts, having consumed too many glasses of red wine over dinner. In their best fake opera voices, they serenaded the open windows of the kitchen. "We know we belong to the land, and the land we belong to is grand. And when we say—Yah! Ay-yip-ah-oh-e-yay!"

Inside, Gabby, who had been putting away dishes, said, "Oh brother, they're at it again. Who fed them so much wine?"

The sisters outside gathered air in their lungs for the grand finale. "You're doing fine, Oklahoma, Oklahoma! OK-LA-HO-MA—Oklahooooo-ma!"

Gabby shook her head, eyes to the ceiling. Then Nate leaned out the window and shouted, "A request from the cheap seats! Sing 'I'm Just a Girl Who Can't Say No!'" And the sisters started all over again. Gabby gave Nate a whip from a kitchen towel.

"Nice going!" She said through clenched teeth. "They won't stop singing until they pass out." But then she softened when she saw Thad sitting at the kitchen counter laughing hysterically. She looked around at the classic movie posters that adorned the kitchen walls. *I am happy.*

Her alarm beeped, rousing Sophie from a deep but restless sleep. For a moment, she couldn't remember why she had set the alarm for five in the morning. She looked around her dark bedroom, stunned and confused. Anything under eight hours of sleep rendered her a zombie. And this morning, she was a zombie who'd had too many drinks the night before. Her throat was still dry from singing the full Broadway musical Oklahoma repertoire. Then it dawned on her—her task was worth pulling herself out of bed with the first tinges of orange just appearing on the horizon.

Sophie barely remembered the shower and she was relieved that she had written a note for her house mates last night before she went to bed. She numbly slipped on her shoes and tiptoed past Bobo and Mitzi who were sleeping in their cat beds in the living room. On the front hall table, she left the note, explaining that she was off on a Wild Ride. They would understand.

XIV

The sign *Farmington* welcomed Sophie. The streets were still quiet of the tourist traffic that would later clog the main street. Outdoor fitters, booksellers, and antique stores stood silent in the early morning dew. Sophie drove slowly, looking for a coffee shop. Wild Ride Flying Lessons was listed in the phone book, but there was no street address or P.O. Box. Her options were to head out to the airport and see if she could find anything out, hunt down the Chamber of Commerce during business hours, or ask the locals. Surely someone would know where to find Eric Jackson. Who could miss him in this town?

She pulled her car into a parking spot right in front of *The Coffee Cup*. She could see several old-timers through the window, sitting at the old-fashioned counter. A good place to start. She took a deep breath and walked into the coffee shop.

Heads turned as she strolled up to the counter and ordered a cup of hot tea. She surveyed the room, seeing a couple of ladies seated further down at the counter. Would it be considered rude to plop down next to them and offer up her sad love story? Perhaps they were the romantic kind. Sophie wondered if she was the romantic kind. *Time to find out!* Her inner dialogue urged.

She took her tea and sat down next to the ladies. She sipped demurely, completely ignoring the fact that the tea burned her tongue and the roof of her mouth.

"Dear, be careful, you'll really burn your mouth!" One of them offered, gesturing to her steaming cup.

Sophie bowed her head and smiled. "Thanks, yes, I'm still trying to wake up." She was eager to rush in with questions. Did any of them know about Wild Ride Flying Lessons or Eric Jackson? But she played it cool.

"So, where are you from sweetie?" One of the ladies, wearing a bright Hawaiian muumuu and strings of New Orleans Mardi Gras beads, smiled at Sophie, expectantly.

"I look like I am from out of town?" teased Sophie.

Both women, without hesitation, said "yes."

"Well, okay, I am a Midwestern transplant who has been living in Bangor for the past few years." She knew darn well that Mainers were like Texans. You could live there your whole life and never become one. The key element in any conversation with a local was to express how much you liked it there. One should, however, refrain from saying they loved the restaurants and the shops. It was much more important to show how much you appreciated the landscape, the people. Luckily for Sophie, she truly did have a love of the land and people—one in particular. She wanted to live here—except for a dream to live in Berlin for a year as a professor—forever.

"What brings you to Farmington?" The other lady asked. She wore winter clothing very inappropriate for the hot day projected ahead. She was ghastly thin, but she had a shine in her eyes. She also pronounced the word as "Fahmington," reflecting the downeast linguistic eccentricities that Sophie had grown to appreciate.

Sophie took a taste of her tea, which was still too hot. How to answer this one? She'd rehearsed what she'd say during the two-hour drive from Bangor, but those words, those carefully selected words, were fleeting. Instead, she winged it. *Appropriate choice of words*, her inner dialogue said, reminding her of its acerbic existence.

"I, uh, I am here in search of a very nice man, whom I met a while ago. I sent him away out of fear. I now hope to find him and make amends. I—I cannot deny my feelings any longer."

The two old ladies sighed, sipping on their coffees, looking thoughtfully at each other. "Well, sweetie, maybe we can help. What's the lucky man's name?"

"Eric Jackson. He runs a flying business for tourists called Wild Ride Flying Lessons. I'm not sure if he operates out of the airport or some private air strip."

"Where did you meet him, dear?" The ladies were really getting into it now.

"At a convention in Nashua. Yes, I know, conventions are full of lounge lizards and predatory types, or perhaps they're one and the same. At any rate, he wasn't like any of those guys. He was a perfect gentleman. He was so kind to me and, I guess, I just didn't expect kindness from a man. You could say I've been through the wringer a few times." Wow, now *she* was really getting into it.

"What does he look like?" Asked the lady in the muumuu, her large chest eclipsing the countertop.

"Oh, he's tall like me and has curly brown hair and the darkest brown eyes you ever saw. He always wears this aviator jacket, and I know, I know, that sounds kind of cheesy, but it works on him, you know?" She said, asking the ladies for reassurance.

"Well, he sounds like an absolute doll. You should stop in to see Mr. Reddick at the outfitters down the street. He ought to know where to find him. And it's about time for his store to open this morning. Why don't you head on down that way and see what he knows about your handsome pilot?"

Sophie took a big swig of her tea. "Thank you very much ladies. It has been wonderful to talk to you and—wish me luck!"

"Good luck!" They said overenthusiastically, drawing the attention of other café patrons. As Sophie walked out of the coffee shop, the two old ladies launched into their own romantic escapades of time gone by.

Out on the street, Sophie shielded her eyes from the sun. It would be just too easy for Eric to accidentally drive by, now wouldn't it? She spotted the outfitter's store, the same one she saw driving into town, and pointed her feet in that direction. Preparing to tell a slightly less-detailed version of her story this time, she opened the door, setting off a doorbell sound.

"Hi!" a booming voice greeted her as she entered the front salesroom. Around her were canoes hanging from the ceiling, life jackets and boat shorts on mannequins, and, in the back of the room, ski's and snowshoes for the other "season" in Maine—outside of fall and 'mud season'—winter. Eric had told her it was his favorite season for flying. He'd regaled her with tales of flying over the White Mountains, encrusted with snow, just across the border in New Hampshire.

"How can I help you?" He said, eyeing her not-so-outdoorsy clothing. She had dressed to impress Eric, not go for a mountain sojourn.

She started to answer, but her voice was blocked by the unexpected gush of music over the sound system. *And when you think it's all over, it's not over, it's not over.* Well, she thought, at least it was one of her favorite bands—Tears for Fears. Her hopped-up-on-1980s-culture younger sister would probably concur. The music was abruptly turned off. Sophie again attempted to answer. Again, music interrupted her speech. *Don't believe it's over, cause anything can happen. Doesn't matter what you did wrong, makes no difference to me. See the light in your eyes and you're dancing free.* Ah, the Finn Brothers, formerly of Crowded House, another 1980s favorite of hers. Was the music trying to tell her something? Instead of "comfort food," was this "comfort music?"

The outfitters proprietor threw up his hands and disappeared into the back to deal with the situation. Sophie was left on her own to wander the shop. To her left was a bulletin board. *Perhaps Eric posted flying lessons here?* She scanned the various advertisements but to no avail. She began to try on different hats, remembering only too late her sister's warning about hygiene—something about hats and lice.

"Sorry about that," the man said, standing in front of Sophie now. "What can I do for you?"

"I'm actually looking for someone," Sophie said, trying to sound casual and not at all desperate. "His name is Eric Jackson. He runs a tourist flying business. Have you heard of him?"

"Yes, yes, he comes in here from time to time to get camping gear. Nice fellow."

"Does he run his business out of the Farmington air field?"

"Oh, no, he actually operates out of Rumford, west of here."

"Oh," Sophie said, disappointed and unsure of herself, "He told me Farmington. Maybe that was easiest to say instead of describing where Rumford was."

"Well now, I might have his business card. Let me see." The man disappeared to the back storeroom again, leaving Sophie to wonder if Eric was too good to be true.

"Yep, got it!" the man announced, handing her a small card. Sophie, glancing at it hopefully, saw that it too only had his name, business name, phone number, and website. Perhaps it was time to call him. But she had wanted to surprise him.

"May I have this card?" Sophie asked, hoping that she had not just committed some small town cardinal sin.

The man looked at her and then smiled briefly. "Sure, take it."

Sophie saw a pair of gloves in the sale bin and picked them up. "And I'd like to buy these. They'll come in handy this winter!" She said brightly. The man smiled again, always happy to have business.

After she paid for the gloves, Sophie was back on the street. The sun had risen over the store rooftops, splashing summertime light on the town. She liked it here. People seemed laid back and friendly, if not a little wary of tourists. She couldn't blame them there. She hadn't heard the term "Mass-hole" for tourists from Massachusetts for a while now but she had picked up a new term at a trade convention: "Citiots," a cross between "idiot" and "city." There would always be a love-hate relationship between crusty Mainers and the city folk who fueled their economy.

She dialed the phone number on the card, her hand shaking. Eric's recorded voice encouraged her to leave a message. She hesitated.

"Hi, Eric, it's Sophie. I'm in Farmington and wondered if it would be okay if I stopped by? Anyway, I'm on my way to Rumford. I'm told you operate out of an airstrip there. Looking forward to seeing you." Sophie pushed the "end" button, sending her message out to the great depths. Would he choose to delete the phone message and her from his life?

"The game is afoot," Sophie said, pulling back onto the highway. Her stomach churned with nerves. She remembered an actress once said she did something terrifying every day in order to challenge herself in life. Well, this was one of those times!

The first thing she noticed, or rather, smelled, was the paper mill in Rumford. It was a sulfur smell, the kind of smell that was emitted by latrines at rock concerts or at school summer camps. Bleak houses dotted the landscape. People wandered aimlessly in the streets because they seemed to have nothing to do. In this town, where might she stop to ask around? Where would a pilot even find a place to fly an airplane out here? The surrounding forests were lovely, but did not allow for much open space.

In answer to her question, an airplane flew over her car. She checked to see if it was Eric's Piper Cub. It certainly looked like it. She was off again, following the airplane with her car, aware of the fact that he might be circling the whole area, giving the tourist who booked the flight an aerial view of the Bigelow Mountain range to the east and north and the White Mountains to the west. Still, it was him! She tried not to hit any pedestrians ("Pestestrians" Gabby always joked) or other cars, let alone buildings. Sophie saw the airplane decrease its altitude and decrease speed. If she lost the airplane now, she'd have to go back into town and ask around. There was an old highway that turned off the main stretch. His airplane seemed to land nearby.

A half-mile down the rugged highway, she came upon a field, not even an airstrip, and saw the yellow Piper Cub airplane. Unable to hide her smile, she parked by the field and quickly got out of her car. She waited for the engine to come to a complete stop before she came near the airplane. As the pilot hopped out the airplane, she prepared to flash him her most winning smile. But it wasn't him. It was some other man with blond hair. Her grin quickly faded. The blond man turned to help another man out of the passenger seat. Sophie waited patiently for the men to exchange a few words before the customer went to his car.

"Hello." Sophie said. "You don't know me, but I was actually hoping to find Eric Jackson. This looks just like his airplane. So…" her voice trailed off.

"Yeah, this is his airplane but he's off in Boston today getting some parts. He should be back by tonight."

"And you are?"

"I'm his employee, John. We take turns flying the tourists around. Today's my day to fly."

"And who are you?"

"I'm Sophie. Sophie Hammond. I'm a friend of Eric's. I haven't been here before and am not sure where to find Eric. You said he'd be back tonight. I am embarrassed to say I don't know where he lives."

The blond man sized her up, a sly look on his face. "Are you that girl from Bangor?"

Sophie, taken aback, said, "Yes, that would be me."

"Thought you never wanted to see him again."

"I made a terrible mistake. It had nothing to do with him. It was all of my baggage. I was hoping to make amends today."

"Did you call him before you came out?"

"No—I, I wanted to surprise him."

"Oh, well, he'll certainly be surprised." The man took out a small notebook and jotted down some words.

"Here's his address. Like I said, he won't be home until tonight. You can tell him that I gave you his address."

"Okay, thank you. I mean, for trusting me with the address. I am a complete stranger, after all."

"No, you don't look strange and you fit his description perfectly." John gave her a wink and sauntered over to a small building, leaving her to ponder exactly what Eric had said about her. He could have used a full range of adjectives: neurotic, paranoid, unloving, cold, etc. The list went on and on in her own mind. And now she had the whole day to wait for his return. Sadly, she had a few history books in the car that needed attention. She found a park in Rumford, sat in her car, and tried to read to pass the time, her stomach doing full somersaults now.

Sophie passed the day in frustrated reading, checking her watch every twenty minutes. Somehow, it seemed like penance for turning away a better than perfectly good guy. She watched the sun set over the trees and her car light no longer provided enough for her book. She gripped the steering wheel, afraid to go forward. She'd done a drive-by earlier in the day to make sure she could find the place. She was ten minute's drive away from possible nirvana or potential dark days ahead. *No big deal. He could tell you to get lost and never call him. No—that's not his style. Argh, why am I having inner dialogue right now? At least I'm not opera singing to myself in my car. But it's probably only a matter of time…okay Stop!*

She was suddenly in front of his house. A light was on in the front room. She could see a form moving about behind the thin drapes. Gathering her courage, she opened the car door. As she stepped out into the street, raindrops began pelting her. *Great! I just spent five minutes prepping for this very moment. Then again, if he can't like me as a drowned rat with raccoon eyes, maybe that's a sign.* She let the rain pour over her as she took the final, brave walk to Eric's doorstep.

There was no doorbell so Sophie gave it her best knock. She sounded like the cavalry busting down his door. She stepped back a bit, unnerved by her ability to practically knock down a door. Then she waited. No response. She waited some more. She leaned over and tried to peer in the front window. Did she imagine the shape moving about behind the curtain? Was she finally losing all of her marbles?

"Sophie."

"Gah!" Sophie yelled, completely startled at the voice coming from behind her.

"Sophie—what are you doing here?" It was Eric, standing behind her. She had been so obsessed that she had not noticed his Jeep pull up in the drive.

Dripping wet, Sophie stammered. "I-I came to say sorry."

Eric stood for a moment, quiet, his head down.

In the few seconds that passed, Sophie panicked. What if he truly did tell her to go home?

Then he looked up, grinning. "How long did it take to find me?"

Relieved, Sophie said, "I had your address by late morning. I was tripped up by you previously saying you operated out of

Farmington. Then I found out you were just giving me a general point of reference. Anyway, the nice ladies at the café, and the guy at the outfitters, oh, and John at the airfield were all very helpful."

"Oh—wow, that's very romantic. You see, I left my contact information with your sister, Susana, with the hope that you might actually want me back."

"I never asked Susana. I snuck out early this morning and left them a note. You mean to tell me that if I actually engaged in face-to-face conversation with my sister, I wouldn't have had my little adventures in Farmington?"

"Yep."

"Oh well, I have to admit, it was kind of fun tracking you down."

"I'll bet! And I have to admit, you look rather fetching completely soaked." Sophie smiled. Then she remembered what was bothering her before he showed up.

"Eric, there seems to be someone in your house."

"That's probably Ellen who cleans my house."

"Oh! Good, I was worried you had an intruder."

Eric moved closer. "She'll be gone soon."

"Oh really?" Sophie said narrowing the distance between them even more.

She kissed him without any fear, self-doubt, inner dialogue or any other strain of paranoia. Eric wrapped his arms around her, molding his body to hers.

"It's too late for you to drive back to Bangor," he said. "You'll have to spend the night. And these clothes," he said, fingering her wet shirt, "Will need to be dried."

"Oh yeah?" Sophie said mischievously. "Aren't you the smug one?"

Eric laughed. "Yes, yes I am." He took her hand. "Come inside."

XV

Susana poured hot green tea with lemon into four coffee mugs. Around the dining room table sat Gabby, Thad, and Nate.

"So, did anyone happen to see the note Big Sister left us in the wee morning hours?"

"Yeah, I saw it. Silly little minx. Knew she'd come to her senses at some point." Gabby mused over her tea, accepting toast slices from a plate that Thad offered to her.

"So, what's the story?" Nate asked, shoving a forkful of bacon and cheddar omelet into his mouth.

Susana was only too willing to go into a full-scale yarn about her older sister's romantic exploits.

"I see," Nate said, gobbling up more omelet. "Well, that's really endearing—but not as endearing as a woman who'll make me an amazing omelet. Might we be accused of being too 'traditional' with our bargain? Are we furthering the wrongs of patriarchal society?"

Susana wrinkled her nose at him. "Please, I cook voluntarily and you fix things around here. In some world, it's okay, I think."

Gabby looked at Thad. "You should be thankful I don't attempt to cook!"

Thad smiled. "Yeah, I remember your last culinary attempt. I'm sure I don't have to ask your permission to be the head cook in this relationship."

Gabby agreed. "Yeah, but I can offer business skills. Just give me your money and I'll take good care of it."

"I'm sure you will!" Thad said shaking his head.

The next morning, Sophie drove back to Bangor. It was incredibly difficult to drive because every time she thought of Eric, her toes curled. There was something tugging at the corner of her brain that she was trying to repress. *No, I'm not going to worry how this is all going to work out. One day at a time. Just take it one day at a time. Do NOT mess this up! Damn it, I'm talking to myself again.* Sophie vowed to tune out her inner dialog, but it remained her front-seat passenger all the way to Bangor. One thing was certain; nothing in life was ever easy.

The party boat was docked on Penobscot Bay in Searsport at the Olde Time Inn. Sophie, Susana, and Gabby were running around making last-minute adjustments to the tables, multi-colored party lanterns, and the music list. No sappy Kenny Rogers love songs were to be played under any circumstances. The Village People, however, were always welcome.

As people started filtering onto the boat, Susana pulled Gabby and Sophie aside." Enough. We've done everything we can. Let's just let the night unfold."

Gabby gently elbowed her. "When does Rob, our pirate man, get here? I've got the life-size images of him for our photo campaign ready at the helm. There are drapes over the images that we can pull off when Sophie is ready to make the brief presentation."

"Oh, goody, I can hardly wait!" Sophie said with mock enthusiasm. "Wait, Susana, wasn't our pirate guy soft on you?"

"Hey, shh! Don't say that so loudly! Really, Nate could be here any minute. I've explained to him a thousand times over that I have no feelings for that mullet."

"Oh, there's Ms. Tabor. She's very eager to meet men tonight!" Susana said, pointing to a woman who had just stepped on board. At the same moment, the deejay turned on the party music, giving the women a jolt.

Sophie focused on Ms. Tabor. Was it? Yes, it was. Jessie. Sophie hadn't heard from Jessie in a while and here she was, all dressed up and looking hopeful. Sophie set her jaw and walked over to her friend.

"Jessie, what a surprise." She said, trying to sound casual.

Jessie's smile faded. "Hi Sophie."

"So, you are now Ms. Tabor?" Sophie said, nudging the conversation forward. She had to get to the bottom of her friend's sneaky behavior.

"I wasn't sure if your sister would recognize my real name and I really wanted to come to this event."

"Why, Jessie, why would you do this?"

"Look. Things aren't any better between Ted and me and I need to feel young again. I'm going crazy. I can hardly breathe any more."

"Jessie, this isn't right. You are still married. You aren't even separated, are you?"

"You don't know what's it's like. Don't judge me."

"Jessie, I can't be a part of this. I'm sorry if I'm somehow violating friendship duties, but I can't help you cheat on your husband."

Jessie inhaled deeply. "I know. I appreciate everything you've done for me but I have to do this." Jessie walked away, driving a stake through Sophie's heart. Susana joined her.

"What was that all about?"

"Ms. Tabor does not exist. That's actually my friend Jessie. Her marriage is in the dumper and she's resolved to meet men." Sophie threw up her hands. "I thought I gave her the sane advice of seeking either separation or divorce from her husband. What was I thinking?"

"Oh, Sophie, you were trying to do the right thing. You can't stop her from making mistakes. Besides, perhaps she's just here to flirt."

"Yeah, I hope so. C'mon, let's go find Rob, Estrella, and Gabby."

Sophie linked her arm through Susana's and headed into the crowded dance floor.

They quickly met up with Estrella, who pulled them over to the bow. "Ladies, I have to admit, I'm on my second apple-tini and I'm really feeling it. Please don't ask me to speak during the announcements, okay? Just acknowledge me and I'll wave my hand." She practiced waving. "At least, I think I can still wave. Wow, I guess that's what happens when a five-foot-two woman, who weighs one hundred pounds, decides to have an alcoholic beverage." She giggled. "Anyway, can you girls help me out tonight?"

"Sure!" Susana said brightly. Sophie was more reserved. "Yeah, what can we do?"

Estrella bit her lip. "Well…you're going to make fun of me but…I kinda like our pirate."

"Who, Rob?" Susana said incredulously. Sophie patted her arm.

"Sure, Estrella, what would you like us to do?"

"Can you find a way to throw us together?"

Susana piped up. "Definitely! In fact, we have some 8 x 10 glossies of Rob to hand out to our guests. Maybe we could set up a table for him to autograph the photos and you can 'help' him. How would that be?"

"Good, good," Estrella said, taking another swig of her appletini. "Then, I'm off until the announcements. Thanks!"

"No problem!" Susana yelled after her, smiling broadly. "I like granting people's wishes!"

"Yeah, at least Estrella's wish is grant worthy."

"Don't sweat it, Sophie, there's nothing you can do. Jesse has to make her own decisions. Maybe all you can do is step back and then be there later on when she needs you."

"You're right, I know. I'm a bit of a control freak."

"No!" Susana gasped.

"Okay, okay. I know I am wound a bit tight, oh enlightened one! I just hate it when my friends don't take my perfectly sound advice, that's all. Jessie's a good person. Oh well."

"That's right—oh well. Now come on. We have a new image to launch." Susana threw her arm around her sister's shoulders, suddenly feeling like the older, bigger sister now.

"Ladies and gentlemen!" Susana said a bit too loudly into the microphone. "Welcome to the first annual Pirate Shirt Dot Com Singles Cruise!" Cheers and applause came from all areas of the boat.

"I'm Susana Hammond, the lovely voice you hear on the phone when you call our office. Now, I'd like to introduce my older sister, Sophie Hammond, President!"

Sophie emerged from the side of the dance floor on the arm of Rob the pirate man. The deejay played "It's Raining Men" by the Weather Girls as they promenaded up to the microphone. Behind them walked Gabby and Estrella.

Susana handed Sophie the microphone. "Thank you everyone. It is my pleasure to announce our new advertising campaign for Pirate Shirt Dot Com. Photographer Estrella Guerra took these amazing photos of our new Pirate Man, Rob Simms!" At her signal, Susana and Gabby removed the drapes to reveal two images of Rob in the Pirate Shirt. The women in the audience whistled and whooped it up in response. Then, Sophie nodded to Rob who removed his trench coat jacket to reveal the same pirate shirt and bared chest, sparkling with glitter that Susana had hastily painted on him.

"Rob will be signing autographs on 8 x 10 glossies over by the deejay. Stop by for a free copy and a kiss on the cheek!" Women in the audience went wild.

"Thanks everyone!" Sophie said, nodding to the deejay to turn up the music.

Susana led Rob and Estrella to the autograph table, Estrella confidently carrying the glossy photographs and winking at Sophie who winked back.

Sophie walked over to the railing of the ship, and looked out to the sky. She and Eric were further negotiating their relationship, but things were smooth sailing. Susana and Nate spent long nights swinging on the porch. And Gabby was planning a trip down to Boston to stay with Thad while he went through physical therapy. She knew that this cherished moment in life was probably not going to last. As she watched Susana and Gabby, who were standing in line for autographs and dancing to "Macho Man," by the Village People, she felt like whatever the future held, they could face it with open arms.

Printed in the United States
69395LVS00002B/19-24

9 781424 153992